June's Troubles
A Larry Macklin Mystery-Book 8

A. E. Howe

Books in the Larry Macklin Mystery Series:

November's Past	September's Fury
December's Secrets	October's Fear
January's Betrayal	Spring's Promises
February's Regrets	Summer's Rage
March's Luck	Autumn's Ghost
April's Desires	Winter's Chill
May's Danger	Valentine's Warning
June's Troubles	St. Patrick's Cross
July's Trials	Memorial Day's Escape
August's Heat	Independence Day's Search

Copyright © 2017 A. E Howe

All rights reserved.

ISBN-13: 978-0-9997968-0-1

DEDICATION

For all of the flora and fauna of Florida's Gulf Coast—
beautiful, endangered, irreplaceable.

CHAPTER ONE

I can't remember what I was dreaming, but it was something too pleasant to be suddenly interrupted by the sound of screaming. My eyes snapped open and I came fully awake, but at first I had no clue where I was. The light was too bright, the bed was too soft and the ceiling was farther away than it should have been.

A second passed before I remembered that I was on vacation while a woman was yelling loudly outside our rented beach house. Her screams had now changed to panicked calls for 911. I jumped out of bed and tried to pull on my pants, almost falling over in the process.

"What's going on?" a groggy Cara asked from the bed.

"I don't know."

"Who is it?" she asked, more awake now and running a hand through her tousled red hair.

I zipped up my pants and reached for the handgun resting on the bedside table. Outside our bedroom door, a loud, deep barking started, adding to the cacophony. "I'm going to find out."

Out in the hall I almost ran into an excited and irritated Mauser, my dad's huge black-and-white Great Dane. The beast did not like being woken up that early. As I rounded the balustrade I caught sight of Dad coming out of his room, looking as cross as the dog. I pounded down the stairs and hit the front door, stopping to fumble with the unfamiliar lock.

Once outside, I stopped to determine the direction the woman's screams were coming from. Now she was calling for someone named Bob.

"This way," Dad said, having caught up to me.

We turned left and ran along the side of the house, then over a small hedge to the neighboring backyard. Built on the edge of a salt marsh, all the homes had docks that provided access to the open water. A middle-aged woman wearing shorts and a sleeveless top was standing on the dock in front of us, looking down at the water just past the point where the sawgrass ended and the open water began.

"Bob, call 911 and get your ass out here!" she screamed again, not taking her eyes off of whatever she was staring at in the water.

She better not be looking at an alligator, was my first uncharitable thought. My second thought was: *I hope it's not a body.*

Dad was beside me as we approached the neighbors' dock.

"Hey, who the hell are you?" a voice shouted from the deck of the house. I turned to see a large bearded man in a robe coming out of the sliding back door.

Dad turned to him. "I'm the sheriff."

"The hell you are!" the man said, glaring at us.

"Not here. I'm Ted Macklin, the sheriff of Adams County," Dad explained in his best *Everything is fine, I'm in charge* voice. "We're staying next door."

"There's a dead guy in the water!" the woman shouted. We all turned and she stared back at us. "Who are you?"

Dad and I introduced ourselves as the big man lumbered across his backyard. "Courtney, are you sure?" he asked his wife.

"Jeessuzzz! I know a dead body when I see one," she

said, still sounding on the edge of hysteria.

"Don't touch anything," Dad told her. "Call 911," he said to Bob in a voice that didn't invite argument.

"Yeah, okay," Bob said grudgingly, pulling his phone out of his robe while Dad and I walked out onto the dock.

When we got to where the woman stood, we looked down to see a man in shorts and a polo shirt floating face down, bumping gently against the dock's wooden piling. At that moment a boat bearing a couple of fishermen roared by in the channel. When the wake from the boat reached us, the body hit hard up against the piling before starting to float away.

"We need to keep it from drifting off," Dad said.

I looked around and walked past the woman to the end of the dock where a nicely sized tri-hull fishing boat with large twin engines was suspended on davits. A boat hook hung nearby.

Using the boat hook, Dad and I took turns holding the body in place as best we could while trying not to damage it. We also borrowed Bob's phone and took pictures to document the body and the scene before the local constabulary arrived.

"Go to the coast, you said. It'll be relaxing, you said," I ribbed Dad, who responded with a surly look.

Eight days earlier, I'd been sitting at my desk in the Adams County Sheriff's Office, trying to tackle some of my backlog of paperwork, when Dad called me into his office. When I entered, he looked up from his own set of paperwork.

"Larry, have a seat. Johnson thinks you could use a break," he said, referring to the lieutenant who was in charge of the department's criminal investigations division. This surprised me because, honestly, the former military officer had never seemed overly concerned about anyone.

"That's very considerate of him. Probably explains why he dumped a couple of burglaries on me this morning," I said skeptically.

"I'm sure it's just his way of showing he cares," Dad said dryly. "Look, I'm offering you a vacation. Do you want it or not?"

I held up my hands. "I'd be the last person to look a gift horse in the mouth."

Truth was, after the last couple of months—which had included a trip to the ICU for me and involvement in a potential hostage situation for my girlfriend—I desperately needed a vacation. I'd been tossing around options with Cara, but we hadn't yet settled on dates or a destination. I settled back in my chair to see what Dad had in mind.

"You know how I always take a week off between Memorial Day and the Fourth of July?"

I nodded. For law enforcement, the summer drinking holidays meant all hands on deck. So between them Dad usually took a week and went down to a buddy's vacation home on Pelican Island to do some fishing and have some carefree time. On vacation and an hour away from Adams County, he could kick back and pretend that he was just another guy having a few beers and watching the sun go down rather than the chief law enforcement officer of the county who had to be ready to respond to an emergency at any moment.

"Yeah, I saw the email. You're taking off next week. Let me guess. You decided to leave me in charge?"

"Ha! Not likely. I'd already told Dave I'd take his place down on the coast like usual, but Genie mentioned that Jimmy was going to be off for a few days and wanted to stay out at my place and ride horses and play with Mauser. I thought, if you and Cara would like to have Dave's place alone for the first of the week, you can."

I was quite touched by this act of generosity. I'd never doubted that Dad cared for me, but he seldom showed his affection with gifts. I suspected he'd had some help with the decision.

"Genie suggest this?"

"Yep. When I mentioned I'd already booked everything

with Dave."

"I'll have to see if Cara can get off. You think the department can get along without us?"

"You, absolutely. Me... sadly, yes." I could tell that his mind was drifting toward the fall election. "Check with Cara and let me know."

A thought occurred to me. "Do I have to pay for the rental?" I asked, only half kidding.

"Genie told me I have to pay all of it. Especially after all the trouble you've gotten into lately."

"You call it trouble. I call it going above and beyond in the line of duty," I said with a grin.

"Get out of here before I change my mind."

I called Cara as soon as I left Dad's office. I was a little worried as they were a bit short-handed at the veterinary clinic where she worked. One of their employees had been on leave since a traumatic set of circumstances had occurred the month before and another had entered the witness protection program.

"I doubt I can get the whole week off," Cara said. "But it's only a little over an hour down there. I'm sure I can get a couple of days during the week and I'm off next weekend." She sounded excited at the possibility. "I'll ask Dr. Barnhill."

Turned out she was able to get three days during the week. We rode down together early on Monday, a Jimmy Buffett playlist setting the appropriate mood for our destination.

"Are you sure you won't need a car when I'm gone on Thursday and Friday?" she asked.

"Certain. The island is small so I can walk wherever I need to go. And I'll have time to get a little work done too."

"You're supposed to be vacationing."

"I went down there two years ago when Dad was taking his usual week and did the same thing. Sitting on the balcony catching up on emails and my reports will be a great way to spend a couple days of my vacation."

I wasn't lying. From the second story, the view out over

the saltmarsh to the Gulf of Mexico was amazing. I could already smell the salt air and taste the beer. *Not too many beers while I'm answering emails*, I told myself with an inner smile of anticipation.

"It'll be wonderful. My out-of-state friends already believe that I spend half my time at the beach anyway," Cara said. "I'll post some pics that will make them really envious."

"I haven't been down to the coast since that last time with Dad. Every time I'm down there, I swear I'm going to go more often."

"Maybe your dad will retire down there."

"Ha! Retire? I can't imagine him retiring," I said, but then thought about the election that was less than six months away. With Calhoun's chief of police running against him for sheriff, Dad's reelection was not guaranteed.

"You sure you don't mind sharing the place with Dad and Genie over the weekend?"

"I'm kinda looking forward to getting to know Genie better," Cara said, watching the pines and palmettos flash by outside the car window as we passed through some of the thousands of acres of woodlands that surrounded the panhandle beaches.

"Mmmm," I said. Personally, I was a little ambivalent about spending the weekend with Dad and his girlfriend, Genie Anderson. On the one hand, some family time wasn't a bad thing, and we'd all been through a lot in the last few months. On the other hand, we'd all been through a lot in the last few months, and I was still trying to get used to living with Cara, let alone the idea that Dad now had a serious girlfriend. I was seeing all of us under the same roof as a recipe for stress.

Cara looked at me and gave my arm a little punch. "Don't be a grump."

"It's all good," I said and realized I meant it.

We arrived at the house before noon. It was a three-story clapboard structure that tried hard to look like it belonged on Cape Cod. The ground floor was all garage, in keeping with standard flood plain building codes. Even the heat pump was built up on a platform eight feet off of the ground. It wasn't uncommon for even a small hurricane to push in a four- or five-foot storm surge.

There were about two hundred similar houses on the spit of land that made up Pelican Island. The only commercial establishment was a small store and gas station with a marina out back.

After quickly unpacking, we set out to live the coastal life. We spent the afternoon out on St. George Island and enjoyed the summer beach experience with all of its suntan lotion and tourist vibe. For dinner, we drove into Apalachicola to visit the Owl Café. Food always tastes better after a day in the sun, but the meals served at the Owl didn't need any help. By the time we drove back down the coast and over the short causeway to Pelican Island, I was feeling drowsy and ready for a nap.

As I got out of the car, I could hear the sounds of an argument coming from next door. As a deputy, I experienced a visceral reaction to domestic arguments. Seldom had a night gone by when I was on patrol that I hadn't had to deal with at least one couple fighting with each other. Now as an investigator, when I dealt with a domestic issue it was usually after it had bubbled over into violence. *Tonight this is someone else's problem*, I told myself firmly.

"Wow, they're really going at it," Cara said, closing her car door softly as though she didn't want to draw their attention.

I sighed. The volume seemed to be on the increase. I stepped out of the garage and looked over toward the house next door. It was similar in construction to the one we were staying in. However, judging by the well kept yard and the more expensive looking trim, I figured that the owners were full-time residents.

The yelling was standard husband and wife back and forth. I didn't care what the fight was about. I just wanted to know if it was going to turn into something that I'd have to call the police about. One thing I knew for sure was that I wasn't going to stick my nose into it. Luckily, just then I heard a door slam and the yelling stopped. Someone had apparently retreated to a bedroom or a bathroom. *Let's hope they stay there*, I thought. I turned to see Cara standing right behind me.

"I can't imagine why two people would stay together if they got into fights like that," Cara said thoughtfully.

I squeezed her hand. "And that's why I love you."

"If you want drama, I can give you drama," she teased.

"Get upstairs. I'm looking for romance tonight, not drama," I said with a leering expression.

"Come on, then, Casanova."

We had a beautiful evening.

After two more days of exploring the coast together, I felt happier than I had in years. I didn't even mind getting up before the sun on Thursday to see Cara off as she headed back to work.

"Tell Ivy I'll be back on Monday," I told Cara after giving her a hug. Alvin, Cara's Pug, had spent the last few days with Dr. Barnhill, but Ivy, my rescued tabby cat, had been home alone and was no doubt highly irritated about it.

"I will. And I'll be back here on Friday."

"Dad and Genie will be here too," I reminded her.

"We owe your dad for the last couple of days," she reminded me.

"Fair enough," I said, stepping back from the car after one last kiss.

The next two days went by quickly. I did manage to get a little bit of work done in between sitting on the deck, watching the sawgrass blow in the summer breeze and walking up to the store to buy snacks.

The bait store and marina was pure old Florida. Unlike most of the houses, it had been on the island since the 1950s. On my first visit to the store, I chose some snacks from my childhood, including Moon Pies and candy that was sure to rot my teeth, and walked up to the counter. A woman in her fifties with blonde hair and skin like an old prospector rang up my impulse buys.

"It's nice out here," I said to make conversation.

"Yeah. I go to the mountains when I want a vacation. One person's home is another person's vacation spot," she said good-naturedly.

"You do a decent business?"

"The marina pays the bills, but the store does pretty well during the summer," she told me.

"Are there many permanent residents?"

"About a third. Vacation homes and rentals are the rest. Where you staying?"

I told her the house number.

"The Jordans. Nice people. They usually spend a couple months out here."

"How long have you owned the store?"

"My husband retired from the Navy ten years ago. A year before that he'd driven all over the state looking for a marina to buy before settling on this one. Lucky for me, his first wife couldn't stand the beach, or maybe she didn't like the fact that he wasn't shipping out anymore. Either way, she left him. I saw my chance and made my move," she said, winking at me conspiratorially.

The door opened behind us and a couple who could have been members of AARP for at least a couple of decades came in.

"Hey, Patty!" the woman said, waving at the woman behind the counter.

"Where'd you get that hat? I gotta get one." Patty nodded to the woman before handing me my bag of treats. "You have a great day now, honey," she said to me.

On Thursday I walked the three miles from one end of the island to the other. With the summer beach season in full swing, almost all of the homes were occupied. I was able to spot the rentals pretty easily, their driveways sporting cars

13

bearing license plates from Alabama to Michigan. I also observed that very few of the full-time residents had children, which wasn't that surprising. I was sure most of the folks who lived there year-round were of retirement age. All of the properties were valued well above the median home price, with most of the ones for sale listing in the half million and above range. The most expensive homes were on the side of the island that faced the mainland, where they could take advantage of protected anchorage to accommodate larger docks and boats.

I stopped at the store at the end of my walk to pick up a Coke and got a friendly greeting from Patty. When I came outside there was a police cruiser parked in front. An older cop wearing a neat but old uniform with three stars on the collar got out of the car. He looked at me in an affable way and I nodded to him. I figured that he must be the chief, and probably the only full-time LEO in this tiny town. *Not a bad way to spend your golden years,* I thought. I doubted that it was much more demanding than being in charge of security for a gated community.

Friday came and company followed. Dad, Genie and Mauser arrived in Dad's truck. His ratty old van, Mauser's usual transport vehicle, had needed a few repairs after its showdown with drug dealers last month and was still in the shop. It had been a tight squeeze for the dog in the back of the truck's extended cab, but they'd managed.

"Where's Jimmy?" I asked after we'd all exchanged greetings.

"We dropped him off at camp. He's worked there every summer for the past fifteen years as a counselor. He'd be devastated if he didn't get to go," Genie said. Her son, Jimmy, had been born with Down Syndrome and managed to live a remarkably independent life in a sometimes cruel and unaccommodating world. "But he loved spending time at your dad's," she added, giving Dad's hand a squeeze.

"He's great with the animals," Dad told me as Mauser bumped into me, letting me know that I should be paying more attention to greeting him.

"What's up with you, you big lout? You aren't going to enjoy the heat," I told the Dane as I ruffled his ears. As though acknowledging the truth of my words, his mouth fell open, his tongue lolled out and the panting commenced.

The house had three bedrooms. I had moved Cara's and my stuff out of the master suite and turned it over to Dad and Genie. It was only fair.

Cara made it back to the island by six-thirty and Genie served dinner at seven—spaghetti with a seafood sauce that was amazing. She was the manager of a high-end restaurant in Tallahassee and had obviously learned a few things.

"This is fantastic!" Cara told her.

"A perk of managing a great restaurant is picking up tips from the cook."

"They tell you their secrets?"

"Our chef is not a prima donna. He's tough with the staff, but I've never even heard him raise his voice. Plus, he's very generous when it comes to teaching others. Our sous-chef started as a dishwasher."

Mauser, pouting because he wasn't getting any handouts, tried to crawl under the table.

"You don't fit," Dad told him. Mauser awkwardly backed out and rested his chin on the table about four inches from Dad's plate. I knew that the only reason Dad wasn't giving him scraps off of his plate was because of Jamie's and Genie's influence. Jamie was Dad's pet-sitter and had helped to make Mauser a little less of a public menace.

"Jamie watching the horses?"

"Yep. He'll be missing you," Dad said to Mauser, scratching his flews.

After dinner we spent the evening on the balcony, watching the night sky over the sawgrass and the Gulf waters. It was a promising start to the second half of my vacation, but everything went to hell when the screaming started.

CHAPTER TWO

The man that I had suspected to be the island's chief of police now stood on the dock, looking down at the body. Clayton Sullivan was in his mid-sixties with a receding hairline. He'd been quick to arrive and had seemed in a surprisingly good humor when Dad and I introduced ourselves ten minutes earlier

"Damn. Looks like he drowned. We probably need to drag him over to where it's shallower," Sullivan said with a Midwest accent. "Chief Sullivan here. We need an ambulance, and could you get the coroner to call me?" he said into his radio.

"You know, he might not have drowned," Dad said.

Sullivan looked over at him, seeming a bit surprised that we were still behind him. Dad and I had followed him back out onto the dock while the homeowners stood near the house and watched.

"We get a couple of drownings every summer. Most likely he got drunk." Sullivan seemed unconcerned that there might be other possibilities.

"Shouldn't you at least go on the presumption that this could be a crime?" Dad couldn't let it go and I could hear the dismay in his voice.

Sullivan looked conflicted. "I guess you have a point." He pulled his phone out and hit a number on speed-dial. "Hey, Sally, I'm going to need you to come in. I know, I know, I'll make it up to you. We've got a body. I'm sure it's a drowning." He looked at Dad. "But you never know, so I'll need you." After he hung up he said to Dad, "I've got two part-time cops. Jack's out in Missouri visiting his folks, but Sally is good. Crap." This last was directed at the water where the body had gotten loose from the boat hook. He managed to snag it again after a few awkward moments.

"You ever have a murder case out here?" Dad asked.

"Not that I know of," Sullivan said, apparently not recognizing the irony of the statement.

"You could call in the sheriff's department," Dad suggested.

"I could... But I always get shit from them whenever I call them in for backup. Duncan is a real asshole. Last year he told the homeowners' board that runs the island that they'd be better off firing us and just letting his guys run the show. Reason they hired me in the first place was that there'd been a rash of burglaries out here ten years ago and Duncan couldn't stop them."

"I know the guy," Dad said, his voice making clear his opinion of the local sheriff. Will Duncan was not the most progressive sheriff in the state, but, in his defense, he worked for a county with a lot of land mass and a small population. He had a limited number of deputies and resources to do a big job. But I'd still heard Dad complain on multiple occasions about how much of a jerk the guy was.

"Maybe I should go ahead and get the coroner out here," Sullivan said thoughtfully.

"I think that'd be a good idea," Dad encouraged.

"Just to be on the safe side," I added. Sullivan seemed completely out of his depth.

The chief pulled out his phone again and called the coroner directly. It took him a couple of minutes to convince him to come out to the island.

"You say you've been the chief here for ten years?" I asked.

Sullivan's eyes twitched for just a second. "Yeah, I'm from Chicago originally. I was looking for a place after I retired. A friend of a friend mentioned Pelican Island to me when he heard that they were looking for a police chief."

"You retired from…?" I asked Sullivan as Dad walked the length of the dock. He was searching the sawgrass for anything that might have gone into the water with the body or fallen off of the dead man.

"The… Chicago… law enforcement," he answered cagily. Sullivan was suddenly paying a lot of attention to the body. "Shouldn't we pull it into shallower water?"

Why didn't he say the Chicago Police Department? I wondered. The obvious answer was that he wasn't retired from the Chicago PD and was being intentionally vague about his history.

The EMTs showed up first and Dad and I had to convince everyone to wait until the coroner arrived. Dr. Thomlinson was in his early forties. He directed the EMTs into the water to bag the hands, feet and head of the body. We all watched carefully as they rolled the corpse over. Whoever the dead man was, he hadn't been in the water very long. The body was pruned, but the flesh was in good shape. There were no obvious signs of fish or other animal predation.

The dead man appeared to be in his early fifties with a full head of grey hair. He looked like he worked for a living with skin that had been in the sun more often than not and hands that were rough and scarred. He could have been a fisherman… or maybe just a casual sports fisherman. His teeth were in good shape, his clothes were of decent quality and he wore a nice watch that was still working. I started to think that Sullivan was on the right track. This had all the appearances of a drowning, heart attack or some other form of natural death.

Suddenly, we were joined by a police officer rounding the

corner of the house at a trot. She was tucking in her shirt and adjusting her radio as she approached.

"Hey, Chief," she greeted Sullivan. "Got here as fast as I could. Chuck didn't want to watch the kids. I told him he didn't have a choice." Her eyes were a bright blue while her hair was short and an odd mix of colors that had come out of more than one bottle. A reddish orange predominated.

"This is Officer Sally Douglas," Sullivan said by way of introduction, then he explained to her that Dad and I were law enforcement and had responded to the homeowner's cries for help.

"I'm going to go back to the house," Dad said to me. "I'll fill Genie and Cara in on what's happening."

The two women weren't completely out of the loop. Cara had walked partway over earlier, but we'd waved her off with the explanation that there was a dead body. She'd nodded and headed back to the house. *Has she already been with me long enough that news of a dead body doesn't phase her?* I thought, shaking my head.

Officer Douglas went over and started to help the EMTs retrieve the body from the water. I was impressed that she didn't seem at all bothered at the thought of handling a corpse.

"Where would missing persons be reported?" I asked Sullivan as the body was carried to the ambulance. Dr. Thomlinson stopped at the back of the vehicle and began to examine the corpse as it lay on the stretcher.

"If the call comes from the island, the sheriff's dispatch is supposed to notify me. Half the time they don't. Not that we have that many missing persons, luckily. But most of the time, regardless of the type of call, they'll send deputies onto the island without letting me know." He sounded downtrodden.

"They gave you this one," I observed, feeling sorry for the man.

"Saturday morning. They're having a summer festival in the next town down the beach. Probably didn't have anyone they could send so the operator called me."

"You hear the calls on the radio, right?"

"No. Sheriff Duncan told me I couldn't be on their channel since Pelican Island isn't incorporated and he doesn't consider me a real chief. We've got a separate channel out here."

Finally realizing where I was going, Sullivan got on the radio with the county dispatch. "This is Sullivan. Have there been any missing persons reports recently?"

"Several," was the response from the dispatcher, heavily intermixed with static and jargon.

"We're looking at a male in his late forties or early fifties. Medium build, medium height. Grey, receding hairline. No other distinguishing marks."

"No one matching that description," the dispatcher told him and Sullivan signed off. "You heard?" he said to me.

Before I could answer, a voice came over our shoulders. "You owe me."

We turned and saw the coroner standing behind us. "I probably should have waited until I got to the hospital, but I went ahead and depressed his chest once we got him in the body bag. The water that came out, I don't think it was Gulf water. I'll need to get back to the office and analyze it to be sure."

"What are you saying?" Sullivan asked.

"The muck that came out had a lot of oil in it and, even in the bag, I could smell gasoline."

"Bilge water," I said. They both turned and looked at me.

"That would be my guess," Dr. Thomlinson agreed. He seemed a bit young and eager for a coroner. I guessed that he didn't see that many murder victims. Ninety percent of the county's population was along the coast—retirees, vacationers and the businesses and workers who made their living off of the first two groups. I figured that most of his dead bodies would be from natural causes, drug overdoses or accidents.

"Of course, that doesn't mean it wasn't an accident,"

Sullivan said.

"True, but chances are that someone moved the body after death," I pointed out.

"Boat could have sunk. He's driving his boat, runs into something, bangs his head and falls into the bottom of the boat. Unconscious, he drowns in the bilge water and the boat sinks. He floats here." Sullivan was trying hard to make the case that nothing criminal had happened. I resisted the urge to quote one of my favorite movies and say, "This was no boating accident."

"There aren't any obvious bruises on the body, though there is a softness to the back of the head," Thomlinson said, sounding very upbeat about the whole thing. "When I get him back to the hospital, I'll take a closer look at his head and run a blood alcohol test and some others that I can do in-house. Try to give you something to work on while we wait for the full toxicology report to come back from the lab."

Sullivan thanked him.

Sally Douglas walked over as the ambulance drove off. "I took a picture so we can ask people if they've seen him." She held up her phone, showing us a picture of the dead man's face.

"You might want to start with them," I said, pointing to the owners of the house who were now sitting on the back deck, looking a bit shell-shocked. "When we got here, the body was face down in the water so they might not have even seen his face."

"Yeah, that's a good idea," Sullivan said. "Come on." This last was aimed at Officer Douglas. As they turned and started across the yard, I fell in behind them, cursing my curiosity.

Bob and Courtney Leonard were looking very unhappy. They watched us coming nearer and, for a moment, I had the weird thought that they might take off running.

After a brief explanation of the current state of affairs, Sullivan took Sally's cell phone and showed them the man's face. "Do either of you recognize this man?"

"No," Bob said. His wife took a quick look and her eyes twitched, trying not to meet anyone else's. Something was going on here.

"Are you sure?" Sullivan asked. I couldn't tell if he'd picked up on the tell-tale signs that they were hiding, or at least avoiding, something.

"I'm sure," Bob said, his voice firm. He reached out and grasped his wife's hand in his. I saw him squeeze it.

"No. I mean, yes, I'm sure," Courtney echoed. "I'm just very upset by all of this."

I wished that Sullivan had thought to question them separately. *Not my business*, I reminded myself.

"Have you seen any strangers recently?"

"No," they said in unison.

"Any boats hanging around?"

"There's always boats. Fishermen. Water's been pretty calm, so there's been a few skiers too," Bob said. Courtney watched her husband and nodded.

"Okay, thanks for calling it in," Sullivan said in the same tone he might have used for a report of an abandoned car. "Give me a call if you think of anything else."

Once we were out of earshot he half mumbled, "I can't believe he was murdered."

"You want me to take the picture around to the neighbors and ask them if they know him?" Sally asked.

"Yeah. And find out if they've seen any strangers. Ask about boats too." Sullivan was still lost in thought.

"Will do, Chief," Sally said cheerily and headed around to the front of the house.

"You don't have any real investigative experience, do you?" I asked, trying not to sound accusatory.

Sullivan turned and looked at me, his hand going up and nervously brushing across the top of his balding scalp. At first I thought he was going to put on a tough-guy act, but all at once the air seemed to go out of him.

"No," he admitted.

"What did you do in Chicago?"

"I was the head of security for a large construction company. I supervised ten security guards. Knew half the cops on the force, including my brother." He sighed heavily.

"How'd you get this job?" I prodded.

"Look, I know you're thinking I'm some kind of lying piece of crap, but—"

"I'm not making judgments. I just asked."

"It's a long story."

"I'm listening."

He gave another sigh. "Same as a lot of guys. My wife got sick of me and left about a year before I was supposed to retire. Financially, I'd gotten stretched pretty thin helping one of my cousins open a restaurant. So when the wife left and took her share, there wasn't much left. She even got half my pension. Never worked a day in her life, but still walked out of the house with half of everything. And when I say never worked a day in her life, I mean in the house as well as out of it. Lazy—"

His face turned red and his fists clenched tight. The man could have blown an artery right there and then. But he managed to get his temper under control and continued, "Anyway, my uncle has a trailer on the mainland not far from here. He heard about the job and told me to apply. My brother suggested I embellish my résumé a little. Some of the guys with the department covered for me when they checked my references." He shrugged.

"You didn't think that this might come back and bite you in the ass?" I was appalled. Half the time I wasn't sure that I was qualified to be a deputy, but here was a guy flat-out pretending to be a police chief.

"Hey! Don't think I don't do my job!" He moved in close, wagging his finger in my face. "What they needed here was someone to keep their property from getting robbed. I done that for thirty years. I stopped the burglaries here. And for the first year there weren't no one helping me, either!"

"And now you have a murder," I said, staring him

straight in the eyes.

"I got a murder. I got a murder. I'll deal with it." He was blustering, but I could see the uncertainty in his eyes.

"You're going to have to call the sheriff for help."

"That's not going to happen. I told you, the man's an ass," Sullivan said and I wasn't sure that this wasn't a pot and kettle situation.

"You need help."

"Maybe I'll call FDLE," he responded, sounding even more unsure.

The Florida Department of Law Enforcement frequently assisted local law enforcement with lab work and advice, but their resources were limited.

"You aren't going to get an agent down here to direct the investigation."

"I don't need someone telling me what to do."

"You don't know what you're doing," I said, wondering if that comment was going to get me punched in the face. I kept an eye on his fists, but he only thumped them hard against his sides. His eyes were narrowed slits.

"What are you going to do, tell everyone I'm a fraud?" There was no whining in his voice. On the contrary, he made it sound like a challenge.

"I should." But for some reason I didn't want to. The man deserved it, I knew that. *But... But what?* I asked myself.

"Jeezus!" Sullivan exclaimed, his eyes going wide. From long experience, I had a good idea what was coming up behind me. Sure enough, Mauser bumped into my ass like a great white shark looking for its next meal.

"Sorry, but he needed to go for a walk," Cara said.

"Cara, this is Chief Sullivan." I had a hard time not putting his title in air quotes.

"Chief," she said, extending her hand. "I'm Cara Laursen."

"Hey." Sullivan acknowledged Cara's greeting but, like most people, he couldn't take his eyes off of Mauser. "That's the biggest dog I've ever seen," he said in wonder.

Mauser always seemed to know when someone was talking about him. He pulled on his leash, dragging Cara with him until he was close enough that he could rub up against Sullivan, who didn't seem to mind at all. He squatted down and started talking baby talk to Mauser's slimy muzzle. I knew that someone could be an awful person and still love dogs, but watching Sullivan interacting with the big goof made me realize that, on some level, I felt like Sullivan was a standup guy. He had done something wrong and was now pushed into a corner, no two ways around that, but I decided that I'd hold off and see what he did next before I ratted him out.

After Cara and Mauser walked away, I hesitantly suggested, "I could maybe consult with you on this case."

Sullivan looked like he was mulling this over and then said, "I guess if you wanted to follow the investigation then we could, maybe, help each other out." His eyes didn't meet mine.

"That might work," I said, wondering what I was getting myself into. "You going to catch up with your officer and talk to the neighbors?"

"Figured I would. You want to tag along?" He sounded as nervous about the new arrangement as I was.

"Let me go back and tell Cara and my dad, then I'll meet up with you."

"Okay," Sullivan said, then slung over his shoulder as he walked away: "Just remember, I'm in charge."

CHAPTER THREE

Cara was just getting to the door with Mauser when I walked up behind her.

"If they need your help, I understand," Cara said after I explained the situation to her. I tried to detect any disappointment or irritation in her voice, but she honestly seemed all right with it. "Genie and I might go up to Seaside and check it out. I think your dad just wants to lounge around here with Mauser."

Mauser heard his name and whined a little. He wasn't happy standing out in the heat and humidity when there was air conditioning going to waste on the other side of the door.

"I won't be too long. I'm just going along to see if I can point out any obvious suspects or areas that Sullivan needs to concentrate his investigation on."

Once inside, I gave Dad a similar rundown. His reaction wasn't as positive as Cara's. "That's a bad idea," he said bluntly.

"All I'm going to do is observe some of the interviews and see where things are this afternoon. If I can give them a few pointers and get out, then it's a win-win."

"If Sheriff Duncan gets involved and finds out that you've stuck your nose into a murder in his county, you won't think it's a win-win. He's a horse's ass and that's an insult to horses' rear ends the world over. I avoid him like the plague at regional law enforcement meetings."

"I'm not going to stay involved with the case that long. I'm just consulting."

"This guy Sullivan has dug his own hole. You should let him dig it as deep as he wants without your help. Remember, you don't have any authority down here. I'm warning you, if Duncan finds out you're sitting in on interviews, he'll have a fit."

"It's not his case."

"Ha, Sullivan won't stand a chance if Duncan decides he wants the investigation."

"I'll take my chances," I said, disappointed that Dad was going to step out of the way because of some bully with a star.

He stood up and faced me as though he'd read my mind. "You need to learn that your bullheadedness is both an asset and a fault. You could have gotten Cara killed last month, taking her out to confront a possible suspect. Sometimes you don't think before you leap."

His words landed like a gut punch. I'd replayed that decision over and over in my mind a dozen times, and sometimes I made the mistake of imagining some of the worst case scenarios. Dad was right and I resented him for bringing it up.

"Now you're going to jump into an investigation where you have no authority, and I'm telling you that there is a real danger you could end up on the wrong side of a man that has his own private fiefdom and holds a grudge. It's bad enough that we're both material witnesses in this investigation. If you're smart, you'll let your involvement end there."

Even though I suspected that Dad might be right, I couldn't let it go. "Sorry you feel that way. I'm going to go catch up with Sullivan and see if I can help," I said, turning my back on him.

I found Sullivan and Sally leaning against his squad car, looking at a map of the island.

"We've talked to the neighbors two houses down on both sides, except your place, of course," Sullivan said to me.

"What about security cameras?" I asked.

"I've found four within a block of the house. They all said we could have the footage," Sally said.

"If he drowned in bilge water, then there must be a boat involved."

"The only rentals on the island are at Patty and Howard's marina," Sullivan responded.

"I called Patty," Sally said "It's just been her and Howard watching over things the last couple of days. That boy they got working for them has been taking care of his mother. She had a mild heart attack and is up in Tallahassee."

"I'm going to go talk to her."

"I'll go see if I can track down any other cameras before I take the rest of the footage home and look it over," Sally said.

"You want to come with me to the marina?" Sullivan said to me.

I rode with Sullivan up to the store. The patrol car was old and musty. I imagined that he must have gotten it surplus. *And probably painted it with his own money*, I thought. There wasn't anywhere near as much equipment in the front seat as in our county patrol cars, so there was plenty of room for me in the passenger seat.

As soon as we were rolling, Sullivan's phone rang. "Yes. No. I don't know who it is. Yes, I think there's a chance that foul play is involved." Sullivan sounded very deferential to whoever he was talking to. Finally he hung up.

"Who was that?" I asked conversationally.

"Ernest Wilkins. He's the richest man out here. Owns a dozen properties and holds the mortgages on a dozen more. Everyone calls him the unofficial mayor, but he might as well be official. He's the one that hired me, even though technically it was the homeowners' board. Most of the funds still come from his pocket. Of course, he was highly motivated to hire me as he was taking quite a beating with the burglaries. Most of the homes that were hit were his. He even told me his insurance companies were going to drop him if the problems continued."

Patty and Howard looked like they were on some sort of mystery weekend. Both of them wore smiles and were clearly excited by the news of a body washing ashore.

"We're glad it isn't anyone we know," Howard said, handing the phone back to the chief after looking at the picture.

"You've never seen the man around here?"

"No," they said together.

"How'd he die?" Patty asked, her eyes wide.

"We won't know for sure until the autopsy," Sullivan said. "Have you seen anybody strange hanging around?"

"Ha! It's summer, Chief. We live off of strangers," Howard said lightly.

"You know what I mean. Have you seen anyone acting strange?" Sullivan pressed them. They shook their heads.

"Maybe someone who was being cagy about letting people near his boat. Not wanting anyone to see into it. That sort of thing?" I asked the pair.

"No... Not really. Just the usual. Add to the fact that we're as busy as a bee in the meadow this time of year. Now, if we'd known there was going to be a killing, we'd have been paying more attention," Patty joked.

"You all got a camera facing the dock?" Sullivan asked.

"No. We've talked about it. Just never got around to it. Sorry." Howard sounded genuinely grieved that they couldn't offer up any camera footage. "Guess we'll go ahead and get one. Feel like I'm closing the barn door and all that."

"Thanks. You all think of anything, let us know."

Once we were back in the car, Sullivan looked out the window without turning the engine over. "There are a dozen marinas on the mainland within an hour's boat trip. Plus a lot of homes on the island and the mainland have their own docks."

"You may have to check all of them," I said, knowing that it would be an impossible task with only himself and one deputy.

Sullivan's phone rang. "Yeah? Damn, Doc, that was quick. No kidding? What about the cause of death? I understand. No, I appreciate the heads-up."

Sullivan hung up the phone. "Dr. Thomlinson did a preliminary examination of the body. He's now pretty sure that the contusion to the back of the head could have knocked the man unconscious long enough for him to drown. But here's the money quote: 'That body ain't been in the water more than an hour, including the time it took us to get there and fish it out.' And he said he removed some more water from the dead man's stomach. The mixture he took out was full of gas, motor oil and fish oil. Definitely bilge water. After that, the boat either sank or the body was tossed overboard."

"So the body entered the water not far from where it was found."

"Got to ask yourself why?"

"You're in a boat and can do anything you want with a body. Why leave it there to be found in less than an hour?" I mused. "Was there some reason the body had to go overboard right then? Or did the killer *want* the body to be found fast?"

"Could be an insurance deal. Insurance isn't going to pay out if the person disappears. Could take years before he's declared dead," Sullivan said astutely. I was learning to respect the man, even if he had lied to get the job.

"That makes sense. The Leonards deserve a closer look. Maybe someone wanted them to find the body, or they might have been the ones that tossed him in. When he didn't float away, they decided to 'discover' the body themselves. In any investigation, always take a close look at the person who discovers the body."

"Yeah, that's what I've heard. The doc also said he took the corpse's fingerprints. Hadn't thought about that. We use the sheriff's office to run prints. I really don't want to get them involved," he said.

"Okay, we can run them through our office," I said. I didn't need a good imagination to know what Dad would think about that, but what he didn't know wouldn't hurt him. I took out one of my cards and wrote an email address on the back before handing it to Sullivan. "Call him back and have him email them to this address."

As Sullivan was talking to the coroner, I called Pete Henley, my best friend and ex-partner. "Pete!" I said cheerily when he answered the phone.

"Aren't you on vacation?" he asked, sounding cautious.

"Kinda yes and kinda no." I filled him in on what was happening.

"I assume your dad is helping too?" Pete said.

"You assume wrong. He strongly advised me *against* getting involved," I said, still sounding upbeat.

"Great," Pete said sarcastically. "And what do you think he'd advise me to do?"

"Hang up on me, call him and report me going behind his back," I said honestly.

"Okay, okay. Email them to me and I'll run 'em through NCIC and the other standard databases," he said, sounding resigned.

"You the man," I told him.

"If I was on vacation, you know what I'd do? I'd vacation. Crazy concept, I know."

"Radical. Let me know what you find out."

"Sarah and the girls are fine. I had a quiet weekend planned. Thanks for asking. Call you later," he said and hung up.

"Let's go get the boat," Sullivan said and started the car.

We drove to the west end of the island and pulled into the driveway of a large celebrity-caliber home.

"Mr. Wilkins's house. He keeps our boat at his dock. Hell, he bought the boat," Sullivan said, getting out of the car to the sound of his bones snapping. "Hate gettin' old," he mumbled.

I followed him around to a gate that led through the side yard to the back of the house. It sat on at least three acres of land, with a large infinity pool in back and a grass lawn that ran down to a seawall and a hundred-foot-long dock. A small yacht was moored on one side and a couple of smaller boats were strung up on davits on the other.

One of the boats, a nice Boston Whaler, had official-looking seals on the side, proclaiming it the property of the Pelican Island Police Department.

We were about to step onto the dock when a door opened at the back of the house. Ernest Wilkins came strolling out to meet us. He was wearing Dockers and a bright colored polo. He appeared to be in his late sixties, and while he'd spent too much time out in the sun, he still managed a healthy, rugged look.

"Who are you?" he asked, piercing me with his eyes.

I gave as good as I got. "I'm Deputy Larry Macklin with the Adams County Sheriff's Office. My father and I heard the woman who found the body and went to her assistance," I said, trying to sound officious.

"I see. Why are you here now?" There was no let up from the heavy stare.

"I asked him to follow the investigation. Of course, I could call in Sheriff Duncan instead," Sullivan said in a polite but less subservient voice than I would have expected.

Wilkins cleared his throat. "Yes, well, neither of us would want that," he said. "We know this is a murder?"

"No. But he didn't drown in the Gulf. He died in the bottom of a boat and his body went into the water not far from where it was found."

"The boat could have sunk," Wilkins said and then added, "But that close to shore, someone would have spotted it."

"I'm taking the boat out to look around," Sullivan said.

"Makes sense. Good luck, and keep me informed," Wilkins said before turning and going back into the house.

"Not much on goodbyes," I said to the chief.

"He's all right. I don't want to let him down," Sullivan said, walking back to the dock.

Twenty minutes later we were in the boat, heading away from the Wilkins mansion. I was feeling very *Miami Vice* with the sun in my eyes and the wind and sea spray whipping around me.

"You make a pretty good skipper," I yelled to Sullivan over the roar of the dual engines that pushed the boat over the waves.

"When I was a kid I used to help my uncle run excursions on Lake Michigan," he yelled back as he guided the boat through the marked channel between the island and the mainland.

When we rounded the east side of the island, it didn't take me long to spot the Leonards' dock. There was no beach here, just long stretches of sawgrass flats. Another island owned by the state and marked as a wildlife refuge lay only two hundred yards to the east, so that when the tides were changing there was a strong current between the two islands. The sawgrass helped to prevent erosion and served as a fish nursery.

Sullivan cut back on the engines. "The tide was going out this morning, so someone would have had to come in pretty close to dump the body in the water and have it end up at that dock," Sullivan said, pointing towards the Leonards' property.

"Is there a chance that it was an accident?" I posed the question as a rhetorical device. Looking around, I couldn't see how someone's boat could sink in that channel, that close to shore, and not have been noticed. Right now, we could see three boats, two coming in and one going out. I remembered almost always seeing a boat whenever I was on the balcony of our rental house.

"Don't really see how. We know he drowned in the bottom of a boat. And he wasn't in the water more than an hour. It just doesn't make sense. Hell, you all should have seen the boat. If it was sinking, it would have drifted the same way as the body."

"I agree. Just to cover your tracks, though, it'd be a good idea to consult someone who's an expert on tides and winds. Also, another boat might have seen something. You might want to post flyers at the marinas."

"Not too many houses with a view of this area. Most folks want to be on the beachfront or facing the mainland for protection from storms," he said.

Not much protection if a real storm comes along, I thought. The whole purpose of these barrier islands was to act as a storm break for the mainland. When another hurricane inevitably arrived, all of the islands would take a hard punch.

Sullivan made note of the few houses that had a line of sight to the area where the body would have entered the water. "Let's go have another talk with the Leonards," he said.

"We don't really have anything new to ask them yet," I said, but then a thought occurred to me. "We could separate them and see if that makes a difference."

Sullivan paused, his hand above the throttle. The engines had been idling with a deep throaty gurgling as we surveyed the area.

"Not a bad idea. Damn, I should have separated them from the start. Just got it into my head that it was an accident. How's it going to work? You not being in your jurisdiction and all."

"You can ask anyone you want to come in and consult on a case. I don't think it will be a problem at a trial since I'm an LEO in a neighboring county." I pulled out my phone and held it up. "I'll record the interview."

"Deal."

CHAPTER FOUR

Sullivan bumped the throttle and pulled the wheel around until we were headed for the Leonards' dock. He expertly cut the engines back as we approached, leaving the boat to gently bump the dock. I got out, carrying the bow line, and secured it to a cleat.

By the time the boat was tied up and we'd turned toward the house, Bob Leonard was coming down the path toward us. He waved half-heartedly.

Sullivan nodded and hitched up his duty belt.

"What's going on?" Bob asked, looking back and forth between Sullivan and me.

"We just wanted to go over your statements again. We've gotten some new information," Sullivan told him. While it was sort of true that he'd gotten new information, by the way he said it I knew he just wanted to rattle Bob's cage a little. *Kudos*, I thought. Sure enough, I saw Bob's eyes dilate a bit and he made a visible effort on his part not to react.

"What new information?" Bob asked, once he'd gotten himself under control.

"I'd rather not go over it down here. Let's go into the house."

"Sure," Bob said hesitantly. "Courtney's lying down. She

was pretty shaken up about finding the body."

"We're going to need to talk to her too," Sullivan told him as we followed him back to the house.

"I guess I can get her up," Bob said, sounding oddly unsure about it.

Ten minutes later we'd split the couple up. I was sitting in the living room with Bob while Sullivan talked to Courtney in the kitchen. The house did not seem as well furnished as I would have thought, knowing how much it had to have cost. *Maybe they're just frugal or don't care*, I thought.

"Let's start with last night. What did you and your wife do?" I asked him. Sullivan and I had agreed to work on a timeline that started the night before. When a murder happened early in the morning, the events leading up to it probably started the night before.

"Last night?" It was clear that the question had taken him off guard. "I don't know. The usual, I guess. We had dinner. I watched TV while she looked at Facebook and stuff on the computer."

"What did you watch?"

"I…" He seemed reluctant to tell me. "Okay, sue me. I like watching the cooking reality shows. The wife tells me that it doesn't help my diet. She's probably right. I watched *Cupcake Countdown*, *Restaurant Cook-Off* and a mini-marathon of *Cake Fight*."

We are not here to judge, I told myself. "When did you go to bed?"

"About eleven."

"When did Courtney go to bed?"

"Later. She always stays up late doing her social media crap. I heard her laughing at some nonsense on the computer when I went up to bed. I don't know what this has to do with finding a body this morning."

"We just need to establish a timeline. Do you remember when she joined you?"

"I don't know. I try not to wake up too much when she comes to bed. Guess it was one o'clock, but don't hold me to that."

Was he purposely being vague so that they'd have wiggle room later? Maybe. Though I often felt better if someone didn't know the exact time that they did everything. When they did, it just smacked of a contrived alibi.

"Did you hear anything or see anything out of the ordinary during the night?"

Bob looked thoughtful. "No. But I tell you, there's always some boat traffic at night. *Not* hearing boats would have been strange. I don't even notice them anymore."

"Did you and your wife wake up at the same time?"

"She got up earlier than me," he said, his tone making it clear that he was surprised by his answer.

"Is that normal?"

"No. No, it's not. She usually sleeps in."

"Do you know why she got up early?" I pressed.

"Not really. I mean, it's not *that* unusual. Maybe she had something to do. She tells me stuff sometimes and I don't remember. She might have been going out shopping or something."

"But you don't know?"

"If she was going somewhere, finding that damn body changed her mind. It really shook us up."

"Okay, so what time did you both get up?"

"She must have gotten up around seven. I didn't get up until almost eight."

"What'd you do once you got up?"

"I went downstairs to get something to eat and wake up, but when I got to the kitchen I heard Courtney yelling outside."

"What'd you do then?"

"I couldn't understand what she was screaming, but I heard the panic in her voice. She gets a bit hysterical occasionally, so I wasn't too worried. One time, there was an alligator in the backyard. I thought she was going to have an embolism over that."

"So?"

"So I came outside and saw her standing on the dock yelling, and then you two coming over from the neighbors'. You know the rest," he said, shrugging his shoulders.

"Can you think of any reason someone would want that body to wash up at your dock?" I asked, throwing the question out fast to see if I could get a reaction.

Bob blinked for a minute and then said, "No."

Was that a tell? Would someone else have been more surprised by the question? It was hard to say.

"You all have any enemies in the area?"

"Not really. I've had a couple of run-ins with people. Had to complain about some jerk causing a lot of wake. Idiot had his boat all tricked out, kept speeding through here a couple times a day. Guess he might hold a grudge. And we had a lawn guy who was doing a crappy job, so I had to fire him, I guess about five months ago." More shrugging.

"You and your wife have any marital problems?"

"What the hell does that have to do with anything?" This was the first time I'd seen him completely lose his composure.

"We have to look into everyone involved with this death. By virtue of finding the body, you and your wife are part of this investigation," I said in a completely neutral tone. There was something here. I found it very frustrating when I was interviewing someone and *knew* they were hiding something, but couldn't come up with the right questions to ask to ferret it out.

"And exactly who the hell are you?" Bob asked aggressively, in what was certainly an effort at misdirection.

"I'm a law enforcement officer, an investigator from Adams County. I've been asked by Chief Sullivan to assist with his efforts in finding out the cause of this man's death. Now, have you and your wife had any marital problems?" I repeated, ramping up my attitude to match his.

Bob looked down at his feet and finally said, "Like everyone else, we've got our troubles. We argue some. We're married, for Pete's sake. Courtney's pretty high-strung, especially when she's knocked back a couple. So if you ask around, you'll hear that we argue. You happy now?" He glared up a me.

"Do you fight about anything in particular?" Having found a sore point, I figured I'd dig around in the wound to see if I could come up with anything.

"We don't fight. Courtney and me, we argue about every dumb thing that a married couple can argue about. Last week I was pissed that she'd bought an expensive purse without asking me. The week before that, she got mad at me 'cause I told a buddy we'd be over for the Fourth of July."

"Did any of these arguments result in law enforcement being called? Before you answer, remember that we'll check the records for any calls for service with your names attached."

"No, nothing like that," Bob said convincingly.

"Are either one of you seeing anyone else?" I asked and saw real anger flash across his face.

"I swear, if you weren't a cop I'd punch you for even suggesting it." This was a lot of anger for something that had never happened, but his vehemence spoke to a strong bond between husband and wife. I decided to change course.

"Think long and hard. Have you seen anyone around acting suspicious in the last month?"

He was still fighting down his anger from my last question. Eventually, he answered, "I can't think of anyone." He appeared genuinely regretful that he couldn't give me a suspect to chase.

"No odd cars in the neighborhood or boats that seemed to be lurking about?"

"We get lots of tourists. They're always doing weird stuff. Getting lost. Turning around in the middle of the street. Half the houses out here are rentals, so you expect to see different cars every week." I had to acknowledge that he had a point.

I wrapped up my interview with Bob and Sullivan finished up with Courtney. Walking back to the boat, I suggested that he might want to pull any calls for service for the Leonards' address and the surrounding homes.

"Courtney didn't have much to say. We can compare notes when we get back to the car. It's a little noisy on the boat," Sullivan said, turning over the engines, which emphasized the point. I nodded and sat back to enjoy the ride back to Wilkins' dock.

We tied up and started walking up the dock. I could see Wilkins sitting on the patio with a drink in his hand. We were still two hundred feet away when I heard the sound of gunfire. I threw myself to the ground as two more shots rang out.

"Get down!" I yelled at Sullivan, who was looking around with a puzzled expression on his face. Finally it dawned on him what was going on and he dropped to the ground behind a palm tree. I already had my Glock in my hand. I looked up and couldn't see Wilkins.

The shots had sounded like they'd come from the side of the house. I got up slowly and started moving toward the back of the house where I'd last seen Wilkins. My head was on a swivel, looking for any movement that might indicate where the shooter was while I tried to locate Wilkins. I could hear Sullivan talking on his phone, trying to keep his voice calm.

I was about ten yards from the patio when I saw someone moving on the ground. "Mr. Wilkins, are you all right?" I yelled.

"I think so," was his hesitant response.

I turned from him and started toward the side of the house in the general direction of the gunshots. A waist-high stone wall separated Wilkins's property from the house next door. I jogged past the house and out into the street. A car drove by and I made mental note of the plate number after making sure that the threat was over and putting my gun back in its holster.

"Anything?" a voice behind me asked. I turned to see Sullivan, his gun drawn and looking wide-eyed.

"No. There was a car, but there was an older couple in it.

Not likely to be our shooter. I got the license number. Maybe they saw something," I said, still turning slowly, looking at everything and trying to spot anything out of the ordinary. I used my phone to take pictures in all directions.

"Wilkins is shaken up, but okay," Sullivan said, putting his gun away. "A bullet hit one of the columns at the back of his house. I called it in. Sally's on her way and someone from the highway patrol."

I gave him the car tag and he called it in. It was registered to a couple from Tennessee.

The house next door was raised like most of the homes on the island, sitting on concrete pillars that were a full story high. Most homeowners closed in the area for use as a garage or storage. Zoning laws limited how the space could be used. Flooding on the island wasn't a matter of if, but when. This particular homeowner had chosen to leave the space open. A white SUV and a red Mustang convertible were parked there now.

I turned to Sullivan. "Go back and sit where Wilkins was sitting."

"Why?" he asked. I had to remind myself that I wasn't talking to a subordinate.

"I want to know if I can see you from out front."

"Damn," he said, seeing where I was headed with this.

Sullivan started down the side of the house and I went back out into the street to stand in front of the neighbor's house. Because of where the two homes were located, the shot would have had to pass across the lawn of the neighbor's house and through the space under the house to hit Wilkins's column.

My phone rang. "I'm sitting here."

"Wave your arm," I told him and started walking around, trying to find an angle where I could see him. It wasn't possible. "I still can't see you. Move to the spot where the bullet hit the pillar," I told him.

"I'm here now."

From a spot on the street, I could just see under the

neighbor's house to where Sullivan was standing. "I got it. Stay there," I said, moving forward and trying to keep him in sight as I walked toward the neighbor's house. Finally, standing underneath it between the two cars, I could clearly see Sullivan.

"Move back to where Wilkins was sitting."

When he signaled that he was there, I tried to spot him and still couldn't. There was no way that the shot had been intended for Wilkins.

"What do you think?" Sullivan asked when I'd joined him back on Wilkins's patio.

"Whoever it was wasn't shooting at Wilkins. The shots probably came from the road. Most likely someone inside a car."

Wilkins joined us on the patio, still looking a bit shook up.

"That's odd," he said after we'd explained the situation. He sounded as if he was surprised that the shots hadn't been meant for him. "So who were they shooting at?"

"Maybe they were warning shots. Just meant to frighten you," I suggested.

"But how did they know he was out here?" Sullivan asked.

"He's right. And if I'd been inside I might not have even known someone was shooting at my house," Wilkins said. I had to admit they both had a point.

"Maybe they were shooting at someone else," I offered.

"Who?" Wilkins asked. I turned and looked at the neighbor's house.

"Blake? That seems like a stretch." Clearly Wilkins thought that shootings were conducted under some sort of hierarchical structure where the more important people got shot first. I could have told him that it generally played out the opposite way.

CHAPTER FIVE

We heard cars pulling up out front and we were soon joined by Sally Douglas and a highway patrolman. We explained everything again. Trooper Mendoza said that he'd go up and down the street and check out all the cars. Sally started to search for bullets. Unfortunately, the column was concrete and the bullet simply put a large nick into it before ricocheting who knew where. A wooden column would have been a lot more help. Of course, there'd been three shots fired so maybe we could find at least one of them.

"I think we need to go see if this Blake is at home," I said to Sullivan, who nodded. He left Sally with a few instructions and then we headed next door.

The front entrance of the house was at the top of a long flight of stairs that led to a rather ornate glass door. Tacky, my mother would have called it. I could hear the TV playing as I pushed the doorbell.

Blake Klein was decidedly average in appearance. His height, weight and facial features all would have fallen in the median range. He was wearing athletic shorts and a tank top, clearly showing that while he was in his mid-forties, he was in great shape.

"What's going on?" he asked Sullivan while letting his

eyes shift back and forth between us.

"There was some… trouble out on the street. We'd like to talk to you about it," Sullivan told him, giving him an *Aren't you going to invite us in?* stare.

"Sure, come in," Klein said, backing into the house. We entered a lavishly decorated entranceway. The house wasn't anywhere near as big as Wilkins's, but what it lacked in size, it made up for in gilt and marble. The furniture would not have looked out of place at Versailles.

"We just have a few questions," Sullivan said, belying his own statement by sitting down at the dining room table. "Sit down."

Offering a seat to someone in their own home was a clear power move. I could see Klein struggling with his own ego until he gave in and sat across from the chief. *Good for you, Sullivan*, I thought.

"What kind of trouble are you talking about?" Klein asked, sounding petulant.

"Where were you," Sullivan looked at his watch, "thirty minutes ago?"

"Here," was the succinct answer.

"How long had you been here?"

"I don't know, about forty minutes or so. I'd gone to the store for some groceries. Really, I think I deserve to know exactly what's going on."

"Just two more questions and then I'll explain. When you got home, did you notice anyone hanging around in the street? Maybe sitting in a car. Or driving down the street slowly. Anything like that?"

Klein looked thoughtful for a moment and then met Sullivan's stare. "No. Nothing like that."

"After you were inside, did you hear anything unusual?" Sullivan asked. I was impressed that he'd asked what Klein had heard before telling him that there'd been a shooting. You tell someone that shots have been fired and then ask if they heard anything and, surprise, surprise, they will have heard shots.

"I don't know. I don't think so. I turn the TV on as soon as I get in the house. It's a habit I've had ever since my wife left me," he answered, no emotion evident in his voice when he mentioned his wife.

"There was a shooting about half an hour ago. It looks like they shot through the carport under your house."

"My God! You're kidding me." His mouth dropped open and stayed there. Good actor or actually shocked? I would've had to toss a coin.

"You're sure you didn't hear anything?" Sullivan asked.

"I… No. The TV was on," he repeated.

"What did you get at the grocery store?" I asked.

"What?"

"You said you were coming home from the store. What did you buy?"

"Food, mostly. I don't know. Fruit. Pasta. Bread. Why?"

"You go to the Winn-Dixie on the mainland?" Sullivan asked.

"Where else? This place really needs some higher-end stores closer to us. I didn't feel like driving up to Panama City," he complained and then went back to the shooting. "No one saw the shooter? Who were they shooting at? Wilkins? I guess that would make sense." He ran this all together like he was trying to form his own narrative.

"Does anyone else live here with you?" I asked.

"Not since my wife left."

"You're retired?"

"No, not at all. I manage Mr. Wilkins's properties. He has several rentals and other homes that he holds the mortgage on. Most of what I do is inspecting the rentals when someone leaves, overseeing the cleaning service and keeping track of the money, including deposits. If there's a problem, I follow up."

"A problem?" Sullivan asked.

"People trash the place or there's something that the police should know about. I called you all about a half pound bag of pot that was left in the house by the marina last month."

"That's right. The Birmingham police arrested the two guys for us."

"Like I said, problems."

"We're going to need to look around your carport for evidence. We haven't found all the bullets yet."

"Sure, no problem."

"Is there a back door?" I asked.

"Elevator. It goes from the carport up to the hallway outside my bedroom. Cost fifty thousand to put it in when I was building the house, but I've never regretted it. Had a knee injury two years ago. Couldn't have gotten into my house without it." He looked very pleased with himself.

We said our goodbyes and Sullivan gave him his card and the standard advice to contact him if Klein had any more information or problems.

"Hey, go ahead and take the elevator," Klein suggested as we started to walk toward the front.

The elevator wasn't very large and, when we got to the bottom, the door took an uncomfortable minute to open. When we finally stepped out, we were facing the driver's side door of Blake's SUV and, farther away, the side of Wilkins's house. It was twenty feet from the SUV to the elevator.

"You take the front, I'll take the back," I said and Sullivan nodded.

Before we started snooping around the carport, we each put on a pair of latex gloves. You never knew what you'd find, and I'd heard about more than one LEO who'd gotten excited and reached out to pick up a piece of evidence without thinking about the fact that he wasn't wearing gloves.

"Here," Sullivan said. He was staring at a bunch of wooden shelves built onto the wall of the elevator shaft that held towels, coolers and other things that you might need for a day on the water. I walked over and saw where a piece of wood had been chipped off the shelf. Underneath the shelf and just above some beach towels was a small hole drilled into the plaster and metal mesh of the wall.

Sullivan called Sally to come over and dig out the bullet and we went back to searching the rest of the garage. When we were done, I got down on my knees with my flashlight to look under everything, including the cars. As I shined my light under an old WaveRunner parked on a trailer against the back wall, I saw an orange object.

I crawled closer, trying to get a good look at it. At first I thought it was a Styrofoam float painted orange, or maybe a kid's water wing. Four feet away, I finally realized what I was looking at. I reached my hand underneath the trailer and pulled it out.

"This is interesting," I said, holding up a grapefruit.

Sally and Sullivan came over and looked at it like I'd produced a white rabbit out of a hat.

"Methinks Mr. Klein was lying to us," Sullivan said.

"Shots ring out while he's carrying his groceries to the elevator, maybe he's even standing there waiting for the door to open. He ducks and dodges, gets into the elevator and drops a grapefruit in the process," I said.

"Now why wouldn't he tell you all that he was shot at? For that matter, why didn't he call 911?" Sally asked suspiciously.

"My guess is he knows the shooter and doesn't want us to find out why he was being shot at," I said.

"Next big question is, is this shooting related to our body in the water?" Sullivan said thoughtfully.

"We don't usually have that much excitement around here. I'd guess that they're related somehow," Sally offered.

"I'd say that's a good bet," I agreed with her.

"I want to go back in there and talk to him," Sullivan said, an undertone of anger clear in his voice.

"Wait until you have some more evidence. We find out who did the shooting, we can put pressure on him to give up whatever he has on Klein," I said.

"Drugs." Sally sounded positive.

"This would not be the worst place to bring drugs in.

People do it all the time up and down the coast. I'd put that at the top of the list. I've got a contact with the DEA. I'll run Klein's name past him and also send him a photo of our body. Maybe one of them will have a record."

My phone rang. A glance told me it was Pete. "What have you got for me?" I asked hopefully.

"Name's Claude Fowler. Originally from Jacksonville. He's an ex-con, all right, but it's been a long time between gigs. His last conviction was when he was twenty-four. Current age, I guess his forever age, is forty-eight," Pete said, sounding proud of himself.

"What are his priors?"

"Assault. Resisting arrest. Drug possession. Connections with some ugly guys. Did two years for his last conviction and got glowing reports from his parole officer. I called around, which is above and beyond, I might add, and turns out he has a heating and air business in Tallahassee. I left a message on the voicemail with your number."

"That's what he's been doing? Heating and air?"

"Until he decided to come down there and die next door to your vacation." Pete sounded very amused by this.

"He lives in Tallahassee?"

"Crawfordville, actually. He's got an ex-wife in Brunswick, Georgia. No other living relatives that I could find. I'll email you her info."

Crawfordville, about thirty miles south of Tallahassee, was the seat of coastal Wakulla County. It was possible that he could have lived near the water.

I looked at my watch. It would be a forty-five-minute drive to Crawfordville from Pelican Island. But getting a look at the man's home might reveal some clues as to why he was floating around down here in the water.

"I appreciate your help," I told Pete.

"So is it just like *Miami Vice* working on the coast?" Pete asked, his snicker just barely contained.

"Don't worry, big guy, I'll be home soon enough."

"Wouldn't have it any other way," he chuckled and ended

the call.

I looked at my watch. Afternoon was quickly stretching into evening. I filled Sullivan in on everything Pete had told me, then said, "Let me check with my family. I might be able to run up tonight to take a look at the place where Fowler lived, maybe talk to some of his neighbors."

I checked my phone and Pete's email had come through with the ex-wife's contact info. I gave it to Sullivan.

"I'll call her," he said. "Let me know what you find in Crawfordville."

I called Cara and told her I was headed home. I was pleased to hear that she and Genie were just getting back from a day of shopping. I felt better knowing that Cara hadn't spent all day at the house waiting for me.

When I got home, Cara greeted me with a hug and a smile. Through the sliding glass door, I could see Dad half asleep on a lounge chair on the back deck with a book in his hands, while Mauser lay in a kiddie pool full of water, already looking bored with his vacation.

Genie took Dad a beer and Cara and I followed her out.

"Back from your new job?" Dad asked grumpily.

"Shouldn't you be in a better mood? You're on vacation."

"All I can think about is the election this fall. I'm feeling like the ant, or is it the grasshopper? Whichever one wasted his time while the other worked diligently. You think Maxwell is lazing away the days on the coast?"

"Let it go," Genie chided him with a smile and a pat on the shoulder. "You need some time off."

"It's not even losing my job that bothers me. It's the thought of living under that pompous buffoon as sheriff."

"Hey, I've got an idea," I said with gusto. "Let's go to dinner somewhere up the coast. Maybe Panacea."

Genie and Cara gave me puzzled looks, but Dad saw right through it. "Why?" he asked. I'd never been able to pull a fast one on him, not even when I was a kid.

"Figured it would be nice to get away from here for a bit,

and away from the spot where a dead body washed up this morning. Just a thought. Also, I want to check out the house belonging to that dead body."

Dad rolled his eyes, Cara looked interested and Genie seemed to be trying to decide how she should feel about the idea.

"I told you, I'm not sticking my nose into this case any further. I'm a material witness. Nothing I can do about that," Dad grumbled.

His foul mood seemed to decide Genie. She smiled and rubbed his shoulder. "Might do us good to go somewhere for dinner. And if we stop so that Larry can do a little investigating, what can it hurt?"

"He's not investigating, he's snooping. Investigating happens when you're being paid," Dad said, but stood up carrying his book. He looked over at Mauser, who'd refused to get up from his pool when Cara, Genie and I came out of the house. "You want dinner?"

The word worked like magic, bringing the overgrown horse-dog back to life. He hopped clumsily out of his pool and proceeded to shake water off of himself and onto everyone else. Now that he was up, he decided to give us all the greeting he'd denied us earlier, rubbing his wet body against each of us in turn until he'd received the proper amount of ear rubs and back scratches.

CHAPTER SIX

We were on the road an hour later. I'd managed to wrangle the driver's seat since we were taking Cara's car. After a protracted discussion weighing all of the merits, it had been decided that we'd go by Fowler's house first.

Cara navigated us to a neighborhood of homes where every house had a large lot, ranging anywhere from half an acre to two acres. Claude Fowler's yard was on the larger end of that range. The driveway ran around the back of the tidy brick ranch home and led to an industrial-size metal garage with three bays. Everything appeared locked up tight as I parked next to the house.

"I'll be right back," I said, opening my door and getting out. I heard the car's back door open and didn't have to look to know that Dad was right behind me.

No one answered my knock and the front door was locked. As we started around the back of the house, I spotted an older black pickup by the garage. Where it was parked, it hadn't been visible from the driveway.

Halfway to the pickup, Dad asked, "Did you see that?" His voice was low and calm.

"What?" I asked as we continued to make our way toward the truck. The garage was about a hundred feet behind the house.

"Someone's in the bushes to the right of the building," he said, trying not to give it away that he'd seen whoever it was. But I saw Dad's hand pull up a little and I knew that he was mentally preparing himself to draw the Colt Commander that was concealed inside his waist band. I felt the Glock resting on my side and started estimating distances to cover.

"Who are you?" came a shout from the bushes.

"We're with the sheriff's office," I answered, not bothering to elaborate on *which* sheriff's office.

"What're you doing here?"

"Come on out and we'll explain," I shouted back. "We just need to talk with you," I added, trying to make my voice as non-threatening as possible.

"I'm not supposed to talk to the police," the man said, peering out from behind the azaleas. We'd kept walking so that now we were only about fifty feet away from him. He was a young black man, probably in his mid-twenties.

"We just have a couple of questions. Are you a friend of Claude Fowler's?"

"Mr. Fowler told me that if the police ever stop me, I'm to call him right away," the man said, his voice an odd mumble that was more pronounced now that he wasn't shouting.

"Did you work for Mr. Fowler?" Dad asked. The man didn't seem to notice that Dad used the past tense.

"I do. I been calling and texting him all day."

I wondered where Claude Fowler's phone was. The ping data could be very interesting.

"Can you come out here? Mr. Fowler never told you to hide from the police, did he?" I said.

"No, sir," he said slowly. There was a moment of thought on his part before he stood up and awkwardly pushed his way through the bushes.

He was almost as tall as my six feet. His shoulders were broad and he carried the extra twenty pounds around his waist easily. His face was open, but his eyes still seemed guarded.

"I'm Larry," I said, putting out my hand.

He came over and took my hand. "I'm Jerome," he said. I realized that his speech patterns reminded me of a retired boxer or football player. I suspected head trauma at some point in his life.

Dad also put out his hand to shake Jerome's. "Ted Macklin," he told the young man, who seemed to have forgotten all of his suspicions as he gripped Dad's hand and smiled.

"Where's Mr. Fowler?" Whatever mental issues Jerome had, he wasn't stupid.

"When was the last time you saw him?" I asked.

"Yesterday afternoon."

"Can you tell me about that?"

"We packed up the van and went over to Mrs. Steven's. She's really nice. Her air conditioner wasn't working and needed to be fixed, so we went and Mr. Fowler fixed it for her. Then we went to a man's house that I didn't know, and he didn't say nothin' to me while Mr. Fowler told him how much a new air conditioner would cost. Then we went and had lunch at Myra Jean's. That's the best restaurant anywhere. I got a hamburger and fries and Mr. Fowler got a salad 'cause his blood pressure isn't good. But since he gets so mad about eating rabbit food—that's what he calls it—I don't think it helps his blood pressure any. After lunch, we went to Tallahassee to pick up a couple of heat pumps we got to install next week. I can lift one into the van all by myself.

"Then we came back here and Mr. Fowler said he had some other work to do, but nothing I could help with. It was Friday, so he gave me my check, and I went to the bank and talked to Marge, who put it in my account. I went home and helped out Mrs. Peters until it was almost dark. I had cornflakes and buttered toast for dinner. I know that's breakfast, but I like it and I was too tired to fix anything else. I watched a show about some people who have to build a house together and they get voted on and whoever is left when the house is done, they get to live there. Then I went to bed. Where's Mr. Fowler?" This all came out in one breathless recounting.

"Was there anything unusual about Mr. Fowler yesterday?" I had to force myself not to go off on tangents like, "Who is Mrs. Peters?"

"Unusual?" Jerome asked, making the word sound foreign.

"Was he nervous or upset about anything? Did he do something he didn't normally do?"

"Nooooooo. I don't think so. I really want to talk to him."

"What's your last name?"

"Martel. Jerome Martel."

"Do you have any family around here?" Dad asked, clearly thinking, as I was, that this young man was going to be very upset by the news that his boss, and possibly friend, had died.

"No, sir. Not that I know of. I was raised by the state and a bunch of people they gave me to."

"You have friends, don't you?" Dad said and I knew the answer that was coming from Jerome before he said it.

"Mr. Fowler is my best friend."

I felt a hollowness in my soul. The pain that some people cause can spread so far and wide. I knew there was no way we could make this right.

"Any other friends?" I asked, saying a silent prayer as I did so.

"Mrs. Peters, I guess. She lets me stay in a trailer behind her house. I got it all fixed up with my posters and things."

"Why don't you call Mrs. Peters and tell her we're going to come over so we can all sit down and talk together."

"Are you going to tell me where Mr. Fowler is?" Jerome asked, his voice going soft as though he already knew what the answer was.

"Yes, Jerome, we will."

Jerome pulled out his phone. After a few questions and answers, he held out the phone to us. "She wants to talk to you."

Dad and I both reached for it, but Dad pulled his hand back. I took the phone and walked out of earshot. I gave the woman on the other end of the line a brief summary of the situation and Mrs. Peters filled me in on some of Jerome's history. He'd been abandoned as a five-year-old child at a seedy hotel in Tallahassee. Doctors who examined him believed that he had suffered from shaken baby syndrome and had sustained permanent damage. Mrs. Peters sounded concerned that Jerome was going to be facing yet another upsetting event in his life.

Dad and I explained everything to Cara and Genie, who were very sympathetic to the young man. I half expected Dad to make another comment about me sticking my nose into an investigation that wasn't my responsibility, but he kept his mouth shut.

We followed Jerome's truck a couple of miles up to a neighborhood of old mobile homes with sagging front porches. He pulled in front of one of the better looking homes with a neat yard and beautiful flowerbeds overflowing with lantana, four o'clocks and night-blooming jasmine. The house was surrounded by a chain link fence that was keeping an excited Pitbull mix from coming out to greet us. The dog was doing a full-body wag as it jumped against the fence, trying to get to Jerome.

"That's Chester. He won't bother you," Jerome explained. It was clear to see that the pup's only goal was to knock visitors down and smother them with affection. He leaped at Jerome, who greeted him enthusiastically after opening the gate for Dad and me.

I'd told Dad that he didn't have to come in, but his answer was a grimly intoned, "In for a penny, in for a pound."

Mrs. Peters opened the door before we reached it. She was an elderly black woman with stark white hair. From the porch, she looked down on Jerome with sad eyes.

"Come on in," she greeted us. Once inside, Dad and I introduced ourselves to Marilee Peters.

"What can I get for you? I got tea, water and soda. I know you're on duty, so I won't offer you a beer."

I thought about explaining who we were and how we'd gotten involved, but that didn't really seem necessary. We declined all of her offers, sat down in her living room and I plunged into the unpleasant story.

"Jerome, I'm afraid that Mr. Fowler was killed last night or early this morning."

I could see by Jerome's expression that he had braced himself for bad news. The weight of it settling on his shoulders was clearly visible.

"But Mr. Fowler is my friend. How could someone kill him? Who did that?" I could hear the first bits of anger in his voice.

"That's what I want to find out. We could use your help."

"How can I help?"

"We just want to ask you some questions about Mr. Fowler."

Jerome looked over at Mrs. Peters for guidance.

"You tell them what you know. I'm pretty sure Mr. Fowler would want you to," she encouraged Jerome. Then she looked at Dad and me. "Mr. Fowler was good to Jerome. He's the one who brought him around here and talked me into giving him a place to stay in exchange for some work around the place."

"You know Fowler?" Dad asked her.

"Sure. He came by a couple times when I was having trouble with my air conditioner. When he found out my son was a Marine, he didn't charge me no labor. Then one day he brought Jerome by. Said he'd been working with him for a couple of months and it turned out the young man was living in an old shed with no running water."

"I like living here," Jerome said with a smile aimed at Mrs. Peters.

"I like you living here," she said.

"Jerome, how did you meet Mr. Fowler?" I asked.

"At the workers' lot," Jerome said like he expected it to mean something to us.

"He means the empty lot by the Fast Mart. Men mostly meet up there in the morning and anyone that needs some day labor, they just come by and pick out who they want. Mostly the jobs are farm labor, building or landscaping, that kind of thing."

"Hard work," Jerome said. "Lot of times, nobody picked me."

"But Mr. Fowler did."

"Yep, he said it was his lucky day. He needed help loading up some air conditioners. He said, 'You look strong.' I said, 'Yes, sir' and off we went."

"Did Mr. Fowler have any enemies? Anyone who was mad at him?" I asked.

Jerome seemed to think hard about this. "He argued with people sometimes. They didn't pay him and he'd get mad."

"That happen often?"

"No. But a couple of times. Made me mad that they made him mad."

"Did any of them threaten Mr. Fowler?"

"Well, they said some very bad words. Of course, Mr. Fowler said them right back at them."

"When was the last time this happened?"

"It was cold, real cold. After Christmas. Don't remember exactly. But it was cold."

"Did anything happen recently that upset or concerned Mr. Fowler?"

"No. He was happy last week. Said he was going to be working his other job some. We might not work every day, but he said he'd still pay me for my days and that I should help Mrs. Peters and meet him at his house every evening."

The mention of another job sparked Dad's and my interest. "What was his other job?" I asked.

"He helped people," Jerome said, as though that

explained everything.

"How did he help people?"

Jerome shrugged.

"Did you ask him about his other job?"

"I asked if I could help him. But he said that it was a one-man job."

"When did you first hear him mention this other job?"

"I don't know. I've been helping him for…" He looked at Mrs. Peters.

"You met him four years ago, and you've been living here for almost that long," Mrs. Peters told Jerome.

"Did you first learn of his other job before or after you came to live here?"

"After. A little while after, but not too long," Jerome told me, and I figured that was close enough for now.

"When did he do this other work?"

"Most of the time on the weekends and stuff. I guess at night. Yeah, I know at night, 'cause he'd tell me in the morning, 'I hope you ate your Wheaties this morning, Jerome, 'cause you're going to have to work for both of us. I'm so tired,' he'd say. He told me Wheaties are a cereal like Rice Krispies."

"Think, Jerome, was there anything else that he said about his other job?"

"Nooooo."

"Did you see any of the people he was trying to help?"

"Maybe. Sometimes there would be a car at his house when we got done working. We'd unload and he'd tell me to go on home. If there wasn't a car, sometimes Mr. Fowler and I would go somewhere and eat supper."

"You don't have any idea what he did to help these people?" I prodded.

Jerome's face scrunched up in thought. "Maybe he took their pictures," he said brightly, as though the thought had just occurred to him.

"Why do you say that?" Dad interjected when I hesitated, trying to come up with the next question.

"Because he had a bag with a big camera in it."

"How big?" Dad asked.

Jerome held his hands about a foot apart.

"He had the bag with him sometimes?"

"Sometimes it was in the van. I couldn't touch it. That was one of the rules, like the gun," Jerome said nonchalantly.

In some places that comment might have sent up a great barrage of red flares, but we were in rural north Florida and nearly every tradesman in the area probably had a gun in his work truck. But even so, my ears perked up.

"He had a gun?"

"Yep, right here." Jerome put his hand just behind his right hip bone. "He always had his gun. I got to see him shoot it twice. Once we'd moved a bunch of junk from around this air conditioner and a rattlesnake was curled up, trying to bite us. Mr. Fowler got it in one shot. Another time, we saw this sick raccoon and Mr. Fowler said the best thing we could do was put it out of its misery. He got it in one shot too."

I had to wonder if Fowler could legally own a gun. Pete had said that the man had some convictions on his record. A convicted felon had to jump through quite a few hoops to get the right to own a gun back.

"Did you ever see him point it at a person?" Dad asked innocently.

"Oh, no. He told me the four rules of gun safety. He let me hold it once. He said, 'You're gonna to be curious, so you better get it out of you right now.' So he unloaded it and told me that guns are always loaded, which didn't make any sense, and that you never point a gun at anything you don't want to destroy, you never put your finger on the trigger until you're ready to shoot, and you make sure that you know your target and that there isn't anything behind it."

"You learned the rules well," I said, impressed. I knew a few law enforcement officers who couldn't recite them that well.

"He told me that if I learned them real well, he might

take me shooting someday."

We went down a couple more rabbit holes, trying to find out more about Fowler and his other job, but we seemed to have exhausted Jerome's knowledge and attention span.

He'd been in a pretty good mood while we talked, but when we got to the door, he reached out and touched my arm.

"I want to tell him goodbye," Jerome said to me, tears suddenly welling up in his eyes.

I've seen a lot of grieving people over the years, but something about the man's innocent need to say goodbye to a man who had shown him a little kindness caused me to choke up. Mrs. Peters stepped forward.

"We'll find out when the funeral is and make sure that we tell him he'll be missed," she told Jerome. The man wrapped her in his arms and began to sob. She waved us on, closing the door behind us.

I looked over at Dad as we walked back to the car. I could tell that he wasn't happy. I thought I was going to get another lecture.

"I hope you're satisfied," he said through clenched teeth. "Now we have to find the killer."

CHAPTER SEVEN

We gave Cara and Genie only a brief summary of the interview, but they quickly tapped into our mood. Everyone was quiet during the drive to the restaurant in Panacea as Dad and I both processed what we'd learned. Dinner at Posey's Up the Creek Steam Room went a long way toward getting us back into the vacation mood. The powers that be had decreed that the oysters coming out of the Gulf were safe to eat this year, so a plate of raw oysters on the half shell served as an appetizer. I received much ribbing and accusations of being a wimp when I explained that all meat should be cooked, but I still chose to abstain and left the slimy critters to everyone else. However, the excellently prepared grouper made it all worth it.

Our stomachs full, Cara and I went upstairs to change into more comfortable clothes as soon as we got home.

"I'll be down in a second. I just want to call Sullivan and let him know what we found out," I told Cara. Then I looked at her and realized that I wasn't being very fair. "I'm sorry about all of this."

"The investigation? You know, you aren't that different from my parents."

"Okay, now you're just getting ugly," I joked. Her parents

were a couple of eccentric hippy types that lived in a co-op down in Gainesville. Depending on the light, her father looked a lot like a Viking, or maybe an extra in a Woodstock film.

"It's the truth. Just like them, you can't stop yourself from helping other people."

"I think it's just my curiosity. I've got to scratch that itch."

She stepped in close to me. "Maybe it's a little of both."

I leaned forward and gave her a gentle kiss. "Thank you for seeing me in the best light."

"Don't get me wrong. I see your faults too," she said, tapping her fist lightly on my chest.

"Faults?"

"Ego is number one," she said, a big smile on her face.

"Grrrrr," I growled, trying to sound menacing.

"Temper is number two," she laughed, moving away.

We were soon involved in a game of chase that ended up on the bed. I playfully held her down and kissed her deeply, then she flipped me over and returned the favor.

"I think we're expected downstairs," I said.

"I expect you're right." She sighed and flopped away from me across the bed. "Let's not stay down there too late," she said and took my hand.

I squeezed it lightly. "I'm feeling ready for bed already."

"Go on. Make your call," she said, springing off of the bed. "The sooner we get downstairs, the sooner we can come back up."

I watched her leave, a silly grin on my face. Then I called Sullivan, filling him in on what we'd learned about Fowler and Jerome.

"So what do you think the other job is?" he asked slowly.

"Dad and I both think he was doing some sort of private detective thing. I doubt he has a license. Pete would have picked that up when he ran the fingerprints."

"Camera, gun and clients that don't want to be known. Makes sense."

"And lots of night work."

"Yeah, that too. I talked to his ex-wife. Didn't get much there. They were married for about six months back in his wild days. They've talked a couple times in the last five years, but she hasn't seen him since the mid-nineties."

"Why'd they reconnect?"

"A mutual friend died. He saw her name on some flowers at the funeral and called her up to apologize for being an ass when he was younger. She said he sounded like he'd grown up to be a pretty good guy. And, before you ask, I did ask her where she was Friday night. Turns out she does stand-up comedy and was working a club in Atlanta. Anyway, she was able to give me the name of one of his cousins, who in turn suggested an aunt. The aunt hasn't seen him since he was a teenager. She was his closest relative and lives in Michigan. She gave me permission to search his house."

"Wouldn't be a bad idea to hit that in the morning. I'm becoming convinced that his murder had something to do with his extracurricular activities. There's a chance we can find some record of his work."

"Bet he didn't report his moonlighting to the IRS," Sullivan grunted.

"The guy had his quirks, but I kinda like him," I said, thinking about how kind he'd been to Jerome and Mrs. Peters.

"I'd like him better if he hadn't washed up on this island," Sullivan said.

"Any luck with the shooting?"

"We found two bullets. One is useless but the other has some of its lands and grooves intact. We could at least make a partial match. That's what Sally's friend at the lab said."

"You still keeping this to yourself?"

"If I can. But the sheriff keeps his nose pretty close to the ground. That shooting went out on the radio pretty far and wide. All it would take is for a dispatcher or deputy to mention it to Duncan. The body hasn't been officially declared a homicide yet, so that hasn't rung any alarm bells.

Sheriff Duncan is more than happy to let me deal with drownings."

"You need to get the ball rolling with the cell phone company to get the ping data from Fowler's phone. Maybe we're dealing with a real moron and the phone is in their boat or the trunk of their car."

"Damn, hadn't thought about that. I'll call now."

Mentally, I wished him good luck getting through to anyone who could make it happen. Normally it was an hour-long process. At this time of night, he'd better make sure his phone was charged.

We rung off with an agreement to meet in the morning and search Fowler's place. Sullivan was all fired up about the cell phone data and was more than glad to get off the line with me.

I had one more thing to do before calling it a night. I texted Matt Greene with the Drug Enforcement Agency. Our relationship had had its ups and downs, but we'd ended on a positive note, so I felt comfortable giving him a rough outline of the current situation and the names involved. He'd be able to check if the DEA had any information they could share. I got a quick reply saying he'd get back with me tomorrow.

Downstairs, I found everyone in a mellow mood. We took some beers and a bottle of wine out onto the deck, where we sat and watched the lights of boats out on the Gulf. The water was calm, with a warm wind blowing in from the south. Despite the lights on the island, it was possible to see the Milky Way straddling the sky. We drank a little, laughed a little and enjoyed a bit of actual vacation.

"I'm tired," I said after a while, feigning a yawn.

"Probably time to head up to bed," Cara chimed in.

"You doing more sleuthing tomorrow?" Dad asked me, only a bit of sarcasm mixed in with the question.

"I told Sullivan that I'd go up to Fowler's place with him."

Dad looked over at Genie, who shrugged. "Let me know.

I might go along," he finally said.

"Sure." Though I wasn't really sure how I felt about that.

Cara and I made our way upstairs and enjoyed some relaxing adult fun. We preferred it with the lights on, so that's how we rolled that night. Little did I know how soon that would come back to haunt me.

For the second morning in a row, I was rudely awakened. Not by yelling this time, but loud pounding. Pounding on our front door. I got up and hastily threw on a T-shirt and shorts.

"Who is that?" Cara asked, trying to cover her head with a pillow.

How the hell should I know? was the sarcastic answer that I quickly bit back. I *really* wasn't a morning person.

"I'll know in a minute," I said, a bit of an edge to my voice.

Once again, I met Dad on the stairs. "Who the hell…?" he muttered as we hustled down the stairs together. Dad had managed to get on a bit more clothes than I had. He was wearing his jeans and a button-down shirt, though only a few of the buttons were done. He was also carrying his Colt handgun.

The pounding on the door was mixed with periods of shouting. I could make out that the tone of the shouts was angry, and they were mostly along the lines of opening the damn door.

I let Dad get there first. He leaned forward to look through the peephole while his right hand held his gun pointed at the floor.

"Damn!" he said. He set the gun down on the decorative table by the door and I watched him compose himself before throwing the latch and opening the door.

"I can't believe your gall!" growled a man dressed like a sheriff, but looking more like a has-been fifty-year-old surfer.

"Stand back and I'll come outside. There are folks trying to sleep in here," Dad growled right back.

Sheriff Will Duncan stepped back a couple of paces so that Dad could join him on the small concrete stoop. I slipped out behind him.

"That your son?" Duncan nodded toward me.

"I'm Larry Macklin," I said, figuring I'd better step up to the plate.

"What the hell right do you have coming into my county and interfering with a murder investigation." It wasn't a question. He turned to Dad. "And you! What were you thinking? Can't you control your own son? Is that the way you run your department?"

Dad stayed silent, letting Duncan burn through the fuel of his anger. He stared at both of us in turn, appearing surprised that we hadn't already thrown up our hands in surrender.

"If you're finished with your tirade, I'll explain," Dad said calmly. "We were asked by a local LEO for assistance in an investigation. We've just been providing that assistance."

"Local…? Are you talking about that trumped-up mall cop they got strutting around here? I let him pretend to be a cop, you understand. This isn't even an incorporated town. He should have called me immediately when he learned that it was a possible homicide."

I suspected that the real reason Duncan tolerated Sullivan was because Pelican Island represented a sizable contribution to the county's tax coffer. Not to mention the political clout that was represented by the folks on the island. Duncan had to face an election in November, just the same as Dad did. Upsetting apple carts wasn't something he'd want to do.

"This is your county. I got that." Dad threw Duncan a bone. "But if you think I'm going to ignore a crime because of twaddle about jurisdiction, then you don't know me very well."

I saw Duncan puff up and thought he was going to come back hard, but before he had a chance to, Dad popped his balloon.

"Particularly when the request for assistance from

Sullivan was backed up by a citizen's request, I felt it was my duty to do what I could." Then he did the name drop. "Mr. Wilkins seemed sincere in his desire to have us help his community."

I swear Duncan's right eye started to twitch at the mention of Wilkins's name. What Duncan had obviously wanted to do was to threaten us both with obstruction of justice charges, but the mention of a man with as many connections as Wilkins had prevented him. Duncan hadn't gotten elected sheriff because of his abilities as a law enforcement officer. He'd played politics from one end of his county to the next, which involved making friends and not pissing off powerbrokers. In this county, Wilkins was an apex powerbroker.

"I'm warning you," Duncan said, resorting to the lowest level of threat. "I expect you to inform me of any breakthroughs in the case."

"I'd think you'd have plenty of people keeping you informed. Maybe if you were a little nicer to folks…"

"Bullshit. I know plenty of what's going on around here. I found out about your meddling, didn't I?" Duncan sounded more and more like a petulant teenager.

"Congratulations, that's quite the coup," Dad said, pushing it a little in my opinion. Duncan's face was getting even redder, which didn't really seem possible.

"Listen to me—" He broke off. "Go to hell." Then he turned and started to walk away.

Dad couldn't resist cutting down a retreating enemy. "So I can assume that your network told you all about the shooting yesterday afternoon? Great! Have a wonderful day." Dad turned away as though he was going to go back into the house.

"What shooting?" Duncan asked, spinning around to face us. I had a brief moment when I thought he was going to draw his gun, but he just marched back over to us, stopping a little closer than good manners would have suggested. "Tell me."

"Your dispatchers didn't think to mention it?" Dad asked innocently, eyebrows raised.

"What shooting?" Duncan repeated, each word stated loudly and with force.

"You know the dispatchers keep a log of all the calls they receive," Dad said, and I wondered if he was hoping to see Duncan's head actually pop.

"Listen here, you son of a bitch—"

Before he could go on, Dad stepped in closer, pressing his advantage. "No, you listen. You came here like a rhino on speed looking for a fight. If you want one, we can go toe-to-toe. But if you'd rather play nice so that we can all do what we have to do, then go our separate ways, I'm willing to play it that way. Your choice."

Duncan chewed on this for a second. He took a deep breath and said, not averting his eyes, "Fine. Prop up that good-for-nothing security guard. But I want to know what's happening."

"There was a shooting yesterday afternoon. Wilkins's next door neighbor appears to have been the primary target. Bullets were recovered from the scene."

I could tell that Duncan wanted to ask more questions, but he wasn't about to give Dad the satisfaction. He turned on his heel and stomped out to his SUV. We watched him climb into a Cadillac Escalade with a huge sheriff's star on the side.

"Compensating much?" Dad said with a smile, then turned and looked me in the eye. "I can squeeze another day, maybe two, out of my schedule. But we need to have a killer in hand soon."

"You don't need to commit to this investigation. I'm the one who started this."

"That should be a lesson for you. Once you start something, you can't always prevent it from snowballing into something you didn't intend. So whatever you thought when you offered to help Sullivan, this is now a grudge match." Dad meant every single word. "Find out what time we're going back to Fowler's place."

When I got back upstairs, my phone had a message from Sullivan warning me that Sheriff Duncan had a head of steam up and was headed our way. I called him back and, after thanking him for the well-intended but rather late warning, I gave him the CliffsNotes version of the showdown between Dad and Duncan. He said he'd pick us up in an hour.

"I feel bad for leaving you alone again," I told Cara, after I'd showered and put on real clothes. I felt like I'd stepped into a deep patch of quicksand.

"You aren't leaving me alone. Genie and I are having a great time together, and we're looking forward to hanging out at the beach and talking trash about you two," Cara said with a grin.

"I don't think you're kidding."

"Heh, I'm not. Seriously, really, honestly, I don't mind. Though you *are* beginning to annoy me with the apologies."

"Okay, okay," I said, holding up my hands in surrender, then giving her a quick hug and a kiss.

"That's enough PDA. Sullivan's outside," Dad said, walking past us on his way to the door.

CHAPTER EIGHT

Fowler's house and yard didn't look any different than they had the day before. Sullivan had called ahead for a locksmith and he was already waiting for us, leaning against his van and talking on his phone when we drove up. It took him half an hour to get in and make new keys for the doors. Once we'd sent him on his way, we stood in the entryway, trying to decide where to start.

"Let's do a walk-through and take pictures of everything, then we'll split up and start searching," Dad suggested.

The house was a haphazard affair. Over the years, several different owners had made various additions to the original brick house. All of the renovations had apparently been done by the lowest bidder and with no grand plan involved. There were a couple of odd hallways and one room that was really too small for much of anything.

I'll give him this, Claude Fowler wasn't a slob. He had a tendency toward hoarding, but everything was neatly boxed and labeled. We found fifteen years' worth of receipts and paperwork from his heating and air business, but nothing that pointed toward his mysterious other job.

"The man didn't have too much of a life," Dad observed.

"I found a photo album from his wedding. He looks

young and, honestly, drunk," I said while going through yet another box of papers.

"Some people grow out of it. You know Elbert, the supervisor of public works?" Dad asked, digging into his own box.

"Sure. I had to go to him more than once when I was on patrol to get signs put back up, that sort of thing."

"He was a hell-raiser for sure. One night, must have been 1988 or there abouts, I'd been called out to a party. Seems he and a couple of pals had decided to gatecrash the shindig. When I rolled up, his buddies all disappeared, but not Elbert. He picked up a friggin' keg and threw it at me. The man was a monster back in those days. It was a Saturday night, so every other deputy had their own mess to handle. I tell you, that was the only time I've been on a call that I seriously considered getting back in my car and waiting for someone else to come help. Ol' Elbert wasn't going to quit. After he tossed the keg at me, he started ranting at the top of his lungs while throwing everything else he could lay his hands on.

"Finally, he got near the fire pit they'd been using and started picking up logs and tossing them at me. I thought he was going to burn the whole place down and, at that point, I couldn't see that I had much of an option but to draw my gun and be ready to shoot him. Seeing me pull my gun just enraged him more and that's when he did the stupidest thing I've ever seen a man do. He grabbed the steel fire grate that had been over that fire all evening. He pulled it back, ready to toss it at me, when his brain suddenly got the message from his hands that they were in serious pain. He screamed like a bagpipe band run over by a tank. Next thing I see is him falling to the ground, crying and begging me for help. He spent a week in the hospital. After he swore to me that he'd never drink again or threaten another law enforcement officer, I spoke to the judge and got him off with a year of probation. As far as I know, he's never broken his word."

"A leopard changing his spots?"

"Nooo, I think it's more that some people have to go through some rough times before they can settle down. That's why I hate the way our system works these days. Prosecutors are afraid to be lenient, or they know that they can't advance in the system if they are. Judges are afraid to do anything that isn't by the book, because if they use discretion and it proves to be a mistake, then they'll get burned at the election box."

I listened and nodded. I'd heard Dad complain about the system a million times. We all knew it was broken, but what choice did we have but to put our heads down and muddle through as best we could?

"I've looked through the kitchen and the garage," Sullivan said, joining us in Fowler's makeshift office. "I'm going to check out his bedroom."

"Good luck," I said and Sullivan moaned, remembering our earlier tour. When we'd walked through the house, the most impressive room was Fowler's bedroom. Whatever else the man was, he was well read. Bookcases were lined floor to ceiling on all four walls. He'd even pulled all the furnishings away from the walls to accommodate the books.

Dad and I spent another half hour skimming the boxes in the office, then I got up to stretch. Walking back to check on Sullivan, I found him on his knees looking under the bookcases.

"I found some blood pressure medication and a few condoms in the drawer. Both looked like they'd been bought ten years ago," Sullivan said as he crawled around, shining his flashlight under every nook and cranny.

I glanced over Fowler's library. His collection covered science fiction, thrillers and mysteries. Mostly mysteries. A lot of them were vintage paperbacks. There were a few hardbacks, including a very nice edition of the collected works of Edgar Allan Poe. Something about the books nagged at me as I went back to the office to help Dad finish up.

I stepped back into the room and looked around at the

file boxes lining the walls in stacks of four. There had to be fifty boxes in the room, and we'd opened them and flipped through the top few layers in most of the boxes. The boxes were like a forest. The paper was made from trees. Edgar Allan Poe wrote "The Purloined Letter" about something hidden in plain sight. We couldn't see it because we were staring right at it.

"Dad, stop!"

He heard the serious tone in my voice and looked up from the open box in front of him. "What?"

"I think the papers for his other business might be right here in front of us."

Dad stood up and moved to my vantage point. "How do you figure that?"

"He needed them to be accessible and he'd want to protect them. Particularly if he was playing at being a detective like we think."

"So?"

"So he loves mysteries. He's got hundreds in the bedroom, and they aren't just for decoration. He has a very nice copy of Edgar Allan Poe's works."

"Okay, so?"

"'The Purloined Letter,' one of Poe's most famous stories, where a letter is hidden by leaving it in plain sight."

Dad's head swiveled as he took in the entire room. "I'm looking, really looking, but I don't see anything other than the boxes we've been sorting through."

"We've opened the boxes and looked through the top six inches or so. When we saw that the stuff was related to his air conditioning business or his household bills, we went on to the next box. But what if he made like a smuggler and put those papers on top of *other* papers?"

Dad nodded slowly. "He'd have a system."

We stood back and looked at the stacks of boxes. We'd systematically sorted through them by starting with the top box in each stack, then moving on to the next one, thereby reversing the order in which they were stacked.

"We've switched the order of the individual boxes, but we haven't moved the stacks," I said. "The most recent receipts were on the left side and the older ones were on the right."

"If I was him, I'd put the newer off-the-record receipts and notes under the older air conditioning records," Dad said.

"Makes sense. That way he wouldn't have been disturbing his recent legitimate business records when he went to access the under-the-counter stuff. We're lucky that he was an older guy and didn't keep everything locked away on a hard drive somewhere."

"Don't count your chickens. Let's see if we're right," Dad advised, moving to the first stack of four boxes on the right.

We hit pay dirt in the first stack. The top three boxes held receipts and notes from his small-time private security business. He'd done a mix of jobs from providing security for an internet sales deal to spying on cheating spouses.

When we found the most recent records, I called Sullivan in to help us, figuring he might recognize a name or an address. We got a bingo in short order.

"I know her," Sullivan said, holding up a note that read: *Received from Mrs. Pauline Schultz—two thousand dollars down payment for int.* The note was signed by Schultz and Fowler.

"She's rich as sin. Her husband was a geologist or something. He bought and sold property for the mineral rights. His health got pretty bad a few years ago and they moved down here permanently. Used to go back to Pittsburgh or someplace every year. She's got the second biggest house on the island."

"What the heck does 'int' stand for?" I wondered.

"Interview?" Dad suggested.

"Intermediary?" Sullivan offered.

"Maybe we'll get a better idea after looking through the rest of this," I said, pulling out another box.

But after an hour, we only had more of the same.

"Where are the case notes?" I asked.

"You'd think he'd have to take notes," Dad said. "Of course, that information would be more sensitive. What we've seen here wouldn't tell anyone much more than who had hired him and how much they paid him."

"They must be hidden around here somewhere," Sullivan said.

"Maybe not. I don't think Fowler was stupid. Some of this sounds like it could involve some real tough guys. Having the notes in a safe place would be important for the security of his clients and his own safety," Dad said.

"He pisses off the wrong guy and—" Sullivan started.

"He ends up swimming with the fishes," I finished.

"Jerome might have seen him carrying around a notebook or pad," Sullivan said.

"And if he did carry it with him, then whoever killed him probably destroyed it."

Sullivan's phone rang. He looked at the name and answered it. "You're shitting me!" he exclaimed and I could see the color leave his face. "We're on our way."

Hanging up, he looked at us with eyes that were focused on something in the distance. "That was Sally. She just answered a call made to dispatch by a boater. They saw a body hanging off the balcony of a house. Sally says it's Pauline Schultz." He turned and started for the door, with Dad and me hard on his heels.

CHAPTER NINE

What they never show on TV is that death is messy. However, the woman hanging by her neck off of the balcony of a large beach house was an exception. She was well dressed, wearing purple silk slacks with a matching purple vest and white shirt and, while her bladder had emptied, she was otherwise clean. I remembered Adams County's coroner, Dr. Darzi, telling me once about a few suicides he'd seen where the people had taken the time to clear their bowels so they'd make as little mess as possible. Looking up at her body swaying slightly in the breeze, I thought that Pauline Schultz might be just that type of woman.

"That looks like good cordage," Sullivan said, looking up at the rope she'd used. I automatically looked out at the boat dock where a small yacht rocked in the wake of a boat that had slowed down to gawk at the body and the group of first responders.

"There's plenty around," I said. "And she's wearing some serious jewelry." I couldn't help but notice diamonds that were large enough to be seen from ten feet below the body.

"The woman had money."

"There's a note upstairs," Sally said from the doorway.

Suicide notes aren't as common as people believe. A lot

of people who kill themselves seem to have tunnel vision that is firmly focused on the doorway from this life to... whatever lies beyond.

"What's it say?" Sullivan asked.

"Not much, just: *I did it out of love.*"

"That's cryptic enough," Dad said grimly.

He hated suicides. Years ago, after he'd had to deal with a particularly grim double suicide where two college kids had asphyxiated themselves, he'd had a couple of stiff whiskeys and told me that suicides were the most senseless crimes he had to deal with. When I questioned his use of the word "crimes," he'd given me one of his penetrating green-eyed stares and said that if I'd seen those kids' parents then I wouldn't have a doubt in my mind that they had committed an act of violence.

After dealing with a few cases of my own since becoming a deputy, I had to say that I agreed with my father. Certainly, in some cases, the person committing suicide has deluded themselves into believing that they will be helping the world by ending their lives, but what a person believes does not change the results of their actions. A man might believe that he has a right to steal money, but that doesn't make it less of a crime. Yes, they may be in pain and not thinking rationally, but the same could be said about a lot of murderers.

"Seems like a suicide, but what a coincidence that she'd kill herself now, just when we find out that she hired Fowler." Sullivan sounded stunned by the turn of events.

"You have to call in Duncan," Dad said reluctantly.

"But if it's a suicide..."

"You can't assume that. You have to investigate it like it's a homicide. And this is a lot different than finding Fowler's body. With Fowler, all the forensic evidence was on the body or washed away in the ocean, so you could get away with just letting the coroner handle discovery. But here you have a whole house. You need a forensic team to come in and go over everything. You need the sheriff's office," Dad said with finality. He wasn't one to let his pride stand in the way of an investigation.

"I hear ya." With a sigh, Sullivan took out his phone and called Sheriff Duncan. After a few minutes of back and forth, he hung up. "He's on his way."

Of course Duncan would come himself. I'd already figured out that he was a man who took everything personally.

Sally came around to the back of the house. "I put crime scene tape over the door." She looked up at the body of Mrs. Schultz. "I hate leaving her dangling in the air like that."

"You did the right thing," I told her. "Officers screw up crime scenes all the time with good intentions."

"I watched where I walked and didn't touch anything," she said, no doubt trying to reassure herself that she'd done her job.

The coroner beat Duncan to the scene, which left all of us standing there trying not to look up at Mrs. Schultz.

"I may as well tell you," Dr. Thomlinson said, "I'm pretty sure that the victim in the drowning was hit on the back of the head. There aren't any defensive wounds, so I'd say he never saw the blow coming."

"Was it hard enough to kill him?" Dad asked.

"Not even close. He would have recovered if he hadn't drowned. Of course, we're still waiting on the full toxicology, but the preliminary tests didn't show much. His blood alcohol indicated that he'd had several ounces of alcohol during the last couple of hours before he was killed, but nothing else."

I looked back up at the body, a thought crossing my mind. "If the killer drugged her, he could dress her up and make it look like a suicide."

"I'll run a full toxicology screen on her too," Thomlinson assured us.

Sullivan looked out over the water, his eyes falling on three boats that were drifting about fifty yards out, gawking at the body. Several of the boaters were taking pictures. "I'll go get the boat and take care of them," Sullivan said, disgust in his tone. Fifteen minutes later, he roared up in the island's police boat, using a bullhorn to shoo the rubberneckers away.

Sheriff Duncan and the crime scene techs showed up together. Duncan ignored us as he walked around the house, looking over the scene. "We'll go in and film everything, then we'll lower the body so you can look it over," he finally said to Dr. Thomlinson, who nodded.

"Don't cut or untie the knots," Dad said to Duncan, who gave him a blistering glare in return.

"Thanks for the helpful hint, but my men aren't as dumb as your people." Duncan turned on his heel and headed back toward the front of the house. Dad shot him a bird.

"Very mature," I told Dad, who just shrugged.

After forty-five minutes, they lowered the body down to Dr. Thomlinson. He took pictures of the corpse from all sides, making particular note of the rope. It had been tied into a perfect hangman's noose.

"Either she or her killer knew how to tie a noose. Had it positioned just right to break her neck," the doctor said, clearly impressed.

"You can learn anything on the Internet these days," I said, which reminded me that we should try to secure her electronic devices if Duncan hadn't scooped them all up already.

"There aren't any obvious external injuries except a bruise on her arm and one on her leg."

"Those look like serious bruises," I said, eyeing the dark purple and yellow marks.

"They're a couple days old and aren't that unusual to find on a woman of her age. Actually, I'd be more surprised if we hadn't found some old bruises."

"Growing old sucks," Dad grumbled.

Thomlinson peered into the woman's mouth and glassy eyes. "I don't see anything that screams drugs."

He finished up and bagged her head, hands and feet before recruiting one of Duncan's techs to help him lift her onto a stretcher and push her back to his van.

I called Cara while the techs were finishing up.

"We came back for a lunch break and to feed your big brother," she joked. I could hear Mauser in the background, scarfing kibble into his huge jowls.

"Feeding the monster just encourages him."

"You're cruel," she said, then turned serious. "Was this another murder?"

"To be determined. From the outside it looks like suicide, but we'll need more facts before we know anything for certain."

"Crazy. Should we be worried?"

"Would Dad and I leave you two alone if we thought there was any danger?"

"You did drag me into the middle of a drug war last month," she said casually, reminding me of how well she'd handled the whole ordeal.

"Don't remind me. I'm still feeling guilty and stupid about that. Dad was giving me a hard time about it just yesterday."

"Don't worry. I'm an adult. I could have said no. I wanted to help my friend and… Things just didn't turn out like we thought, but all's well that ends well."

"I appreciate the Bard's seal of approval," I said, smiling into the phone. Then I saw Duncan come around the corner of the house, striding purposefully toward us with a frown on his face. "I've got to go. The bad news sheriff is headed our way."

"Suicide," Duncan said bluntly. "A waste of time. Anyone should have been able to take a look at the scene and known what the score was." He hit Sullivan with the high beams. "Of course, if most of your experience is giving out parking tickets and open container citations, then I guess you can't be expected to recognize these things."

"Don't you want to wait until the toxicology report comes back before you make any grand declarations?" Dad asked, goading him.

"Tell you what. I'm giving this one to you all to handle. Meanwhile, I'll be looking into the Fowler murder." Sullivan started to say something, but Duncan cut him off. "Don't try and threaten me with your fairy godfather either. I'm sure he'll be fine with both of us working the case. If you solve it, good for you. But I'm going to investigate it and I'm betting I get over the goal line before you and your out-of-town ringers." He turned and walked away.

"Bastard," Dad said when Duncan was out of earshot.

The three of us walked through the house after Duncan's crime scene techs had packed up and left. From the look of the house, they'd done a decent job of dusting for prints and collecting evidence. But the proof would be in the investigation, which I didn't have any faith in since Duncan had already declared it over.

We found a present from Duncan sitting on the dining room table. Piled up were a desktop computer, laptop, an iPad and three cell phones. A note from Duncan had been placed on top of them. The note read: *She junked them before she offed herself. P.S.—There weren't any fingerprints.*

"Damn," Sullivan said, looking at the laptop and the holes that had been drilled through it. The desktop casing was off and the hard drive had been pulled and drilled. The iPad had also received the drill routine, while the cell phones had had their SIM cards pulled and no doubt their memories flushed.

"Not going to get much out of this," Dad said. "But at her age... It seems surprising that she knew how to do all this." He indicated the pile of landfill fodder on the table.

"YouTube," I said. "You can learn how to do anything on YouTube."

"You aren't going to learn how to pull information from a drilled hard drive," Sally said, poking the desktop.

"True, and we aren't going to learn what she researched from this pile of junk either. She really wanted to make a clean go of it," I sighed.

"It's possible someone else did all of this," Dad said.

"Going to be hard to prove. Which is why Duncan tossed it to me."

"I'd call him on it and get whatever reports you can from the crime scene techs," I told Sullivan.

"I will. There are a couple of people working in the office who are all right. They'll give me what they can."

"Let's go through the rest of the house," Dad said.

"Look for a drill," I suggested. If we didn't find a drill then it might have meant someone else had destroyed the electronics.

We decided to look through the house as a group so that we could discuss what we were seeing. The house was immaculate except for the mess left by Duncan's people. The furniture was top of the line, but not tacky like Klein's.

"Did you notice anything out of place or unusual when you discovered the body?" I asked Sally as we walked.

"No. The note was sitting on a pillow on the bed. I leaned over and read it, that's all. I noticed the rope and went out on the balcony and saw Mrs. Schultz hanging there. I could tell it was too late to help her, so I called you," she said to Sullivan. "Then I finished walking through the house. Place was neat as a pin."

"I've got a drill!" Dad shouted after a while, emerging from a walk-in utility closet. "Looks like they dusted it for prints."

In the kitchen, I opened the trash can. There was nothing inside, not even a trash liner.

Dad looked at me, then over at Sullivan. "When do they pick up the trash?"

"Tomorrow."

We all traipsed outside and opened the large plastic trash bin hidden in an alcove on the side of the house. Inside were several bags of trash.

"Duncan's team could use some additional training," Dad said smugly. "Checking the garbage is SOP."

We spent the next half hour picking through and analyzing Schultz's trash. The bag on top wasn't very interesting.

"This is the bag from the kitchen," I said, stating the obvious as we looked at banana peels and various food wrappers and cartons.

"Honing your deductive powers, Sherlock?" Dad joked. He was in a better mood since we had discovered that Duncan's team dropped an important ball.

"What do you think?" Sullivan asked us.

"My dad's sarcasm aside, I think that someone who takes out the garbage before they hang themselves is pretty determined to set all of their affairs in order before they die."

"I admit that I can't see any reason why a killer would have thrown this out. I'd hoped to find something incriminating. You'd be surprised how many crooks toss things in the garbage like it's a magic bin that will make the evidence disappear," Dad said.

The last bag in the bin left us with a puzzle, figuratively and literally. Inside was a very large ball of shredded paper.

"She certainly cleaned house," Sally said, gingerly picking at the strips of paper tangled together to form a ball about two feet in diameter.

"This is looking more and more like a suicide," Dad admitted.

"But why now? What did she hire Fowler to do? And is this," I indicated the ball of paper, "an indication that she was trying to hide something?"

"All good questions," Dad said.

We all stared at the ball of paper, knowing what was coming next.

"Lot of work trying to put Humpty Dumpty together again," Sally said.

Dad picked up the bag. "Let's take it back to our place. We'll see if we can at least get some key words off of it that might give us a hint what was going on."

CHAPTER TEN

We introduced Sullivan and Sally to Genie, Cara and Mauser. Mauser was thrilled to have company and preformed his "I'm an idiot" act to perfection. He was fascinated with the pile of shredded paper, grabbing a piece and having a grand time as we chased him around the living room trying to get it back.

After eventually bribing Mauser with a peanut-butter-filled Kong to leave us alone, we all stood around the dining room table, staring at the strips of paper and wondering where to begin.

"What a mess," was Cara's succinct evaluation of the situation as she reached out to pull pieces from the pile and place them into groups.

"I've always liked puzzles," Genie said, starting her own pile.

"I don't have much hope of reconstructing the documents, but if we could at least glean some key words out of them, that might help," Dad said.

"At least she had one of the older model home shredders. This is doable," I said, trying to sound upbeat while secretly hoping that one of the others would take the lead on the mind-boggling task.

"If Genie and Cara don't mind, let's let them group the pieces together as best they can, then we'll read through the groups," Sullivan suggested.

"The trick is going to be gauging the right amount of wine to have. Too much and we'll go to sleep or start laughing hysterically. Too little and the boredom will overwhelm us," Genie said, nudging Cara, who nudged her back with a smile. At that moment I wondered if Dad and I weren't making a big mistake letting the two of them spend so much time together.

"At least there are some different shades and types of paper," Sally said, picking up a few pieces that appeared to be from a yellow legal pad and putting them into a pile that Cara had started.

After a few minutes of getting in Cara's and Genie's way, the rest of us walked away from the table to strategize the next steps in the investigation. We were joined by Mauser, who'd managed to obliterate half a cup of peanut butter in record time.

"As much as I'd like to, we can't treat Duncan and his people as adversaries," Dad said, scratching Mauser's ears.

"Duncan's an ass, but he has resources and a right to investigate the murder," Sullivan agreed.

"And Mr. Fowler doesn't need us fighting over whose case this is," Sally said.

"Which doesn't mean we have to share everything with them." I was perfectly willing to stick my neck out on the obstruction of justice limb. I was a bit surprised when I didn't get a dirty look from Dad, but he had been known to dodge a point of law from time to time himself.

"If we're agreed that we won't hold anything back that Duncan's people could make better use of, and we only withhold information for a reasonable amount of time—" Dad started.

"Reasonable?" Sally questioned him before I had the chance.

"That will be determined on a case-by-case basis."

"Don't you have to get back to work?" Sullivan aimed this question at both Dad and me. Dad looked grim as he considered.

"We can both give you two more days. But I'll have to be back at work on Wednesday morning. I'll consider extending Larry's time off when we get to that point," Dad finally said, determined to get the job done.

"I appreciate what you're doing for us," Sullivan said.

"So what do we need to do now?" Sally asked.

"There are several possibilities," Dad began.

"One is that the body, the shooting and the hanging are all related," I said.

"True. But related doesn't necessarily mean that they were committed by the same person," Dad pointed out.

"Of course, one of them could be an outlier," Sullivan said thoughtfully.

"Or none of them are related and it's all just a bunch of stuff that happened. But on this island…" Sally shook her head. "That doesn't seem very likely."

Dad nodded. "I think we all agree with you there. So let's go with the assumption that at least two of the incidents are connected. Finding the things that bind them together will help us to determine what other elements are tied to those events."

"We already have one tie that binds. Fowler was hired by Pauline," I threw out.

"There's solid evidence that that's the case. Okay, so why did Pauline hire him? Was he killed because of the job that she hired him to do?"

"The shredded documents could answer the first question," Sullivan said, nodding to the table where Cara and Genie were buried up to their elbows in paper snakes.

"And we're happy to sacrifice our time on the beach to help out," Genie said good-naturedly, not looking up from the thousands of strips of paper.

"I think we should assume that Fowler was killed because of Pauline's job," I said.

"Why?" Dad tossed back.

"The body was found on the same small island where Pauline lived. And I think it's possible that if, and it's a big if, she killed herself, then the connection still makes sense. She hires someone out of desperation. He winds up dead. She's now left with no option but to kill herself."

"The first part is good circumstantial evidence. The second is speculation. Logical speculation, but there could be a dozen other ways in which the events could be connected. For example, maybe she hired Fowler to protect her. The threat eliminates Fowler, then kills Schultz," Dad challenged me.

"*If* Schultz's death is murder," Sally said.

"Or if, like Larry said, she killed herself because she was now defenseless without Fowler."

"What about the shooting?" Sullivan asked. "How does that fit in?"

"Maybe it doesn't. Yes or no, finding that out would give the investigation a real boost," I admitted.

"Here's something odd," Sullivan said, pulling his phone out of its case, glancing at it and then putting it back. "I called Mrs. Schultz's son and left a message hours ago, but I haven't heard back."

"He didn't get it?" I suggested.

"Or he put his phone on vibrate and hasn't noticed. It *is* Sunday," Sally pointed out.

"Maybe."

"Do you know anything about her son?" Dad asked.

"He's from a previous marriage. Lives in New York. One of the neighbors gave Sally the information."

"Mr. Henderson lives next door. Mrs. Schultz gave him her son's name and number after Mr. Schultz died. She would go on trips and Henderson would watch the house, that sort of thing. She told him not to call the son unless it was an extreme emergency. He said she emphasized the word 'extreme,'" Sally said.

"Guess they weren't a tight family," I said.

"How much did you question the neighbors?" Dad asked Sally.

"Just asked them if they saw or heard anything unusual. Most of the neighbors knew Mrs. Schultz, so I asked them when they'd last seen her and if she'd been acting any different." Sally took out a small pad and looked at her notes. "The last person to report seeing her was her neighbor across the street. She said she saw her yesterday afternoon. Mrs. Schultz had just come back from the mainland and was checking her mail."

"Canvassing the neighbors again would be a good idea. This time we should be looking for anything in Mrs. Schultz's life that stands out," Dad said.

"Like what?" Sally asked.

"Visitors. Was there anybody that visited her on a regular basis? Who were her friends? Did any of the neighbors see Fowler? We've got his DMV photo now; we can show that around. Did her behavior change in the last few weeks or months? We need to find out what happened that caused her to hire Fowler." As Dad talked, Sally took notes.

"I think we need to talk to the Leonards again. Something about them doesn't seem right," I said.

"There was definitely an evasiveness. But that could be due to a lot of things," Dad said. "Worth a little digging."

He was right. Witnesses have their own agendas too. I'd had a rape case about a year ago where a twenty-five-year-old neighbor was so evasive and secretive that I had started to focus on him as a suspect. He didn't want to tell me anything about how he spent his time, lawyered up at the first opportunity and was seen burning something in his backyard in the middle of the night. Turned out that he'd been hiding ten pot plants in a small grow room. When I finally discovered that he'd wasted my time, I came back after solving the rape and prosecuted him for everything I could.

My phone and Sullivan's went off at the same time. My call was from Matt. Always the workaholic, he'd gone into his office and checked everything he could find concerning drugs in the Pelican Island area.

"Nothing notable and nothing involving the names you gave me. We try and monitor all the local marinas, but it's tough. Especially when using local law enforcement is problematic."

"Because of corruption," I said, more a statement than a question. I could name a dozen big busts that had exposed local law enforcement officers who were involved in drug smuggling. Drug smugglers could almost always find an officer who could be bribed or blackmailed into helping them or, at the very least, looking the other way.

"I imagine fifty percent of the docks in Florida, public and private, have seen some drugs come in through them. But nothing in the area is on a watch list and none of the names have red flags next to them."

"I appreciate you checking."

"I'm going to be in your neck of the woods next month."

"The Thompson hearings?" I asked, referring to a large case involving racketeering and drug dealing in Adams County. I was working the case for the sheriff's office and had already given a couple of depositions on the numerous charges.

"I've been assigned as the DEA's lead investigator on the case."

"Glad to hear it. We'll have lunch," I said.

Until recently, I wouldn't have been so pleased to have him back in the county. He and I hadn't gotten along very well when we were working side by side, but a lot of water had passed under the bridge since then.

Sullivan and I hung up about the same time. I told everyone what Matt had told me before Sullivan reported that he'd been talking to Mrs. Schultz's son.

"Not a lot of love there. He's already spoken to the neighbor. The son told me he didn't care what happened to the body. But he said he was flying down this evening and staying a week to take care of the property."

"Did he believe that she'd committed suicide?" Sally

asked. Family members will often find it harder to accept a suicide than a murder.

"He said, and this is pretty much a direct quote, 'Who knows what the hell she might do.'"

"That's cold," Sally said.

"Makes you wonder where he was when she died. Chances are he stands to inherit a lot of money," I said.

"I asked him that since he wasn't acting like a grieving relative. Said he had plenty of witnesses. He was at a family wedding. I asked him to bring me contact information for some of the witnesses and he said that wouldn't be a problem." Sullivan shrugged.

"Maybe he hired someone. They were stalking Schultz, she got wind of it and hired Fowler to find out who was lurking in the bushes. The hitman takes out Fowler *and* Schultz," Dad offered.

"Plausible," I said and got a little smile from Dad. "But we still aren't sure that Schultz was murdered."

"I can't decide whether I'm rooting for a determination of suicide or homicide," Dad said. "Suicide would push the narrative one direction while homicide would push it another way."

"We've managed to sort this into some general groups," Cara called over to us.

On the table there were seven groups of shredded paper, separated by the type of paper. The two biggest piles were made up of ordinary copy paper and sheets of yellow legal paper.

"Looks like she got in a rush and put some of the paper in sideways," Genie said, pointing to subsets of the different piles. "Going in that way, you almost have some complete sentences."

We each started looking through the piles. At one point, Cara left to find us some blank notepads so we could write down the words that were legible.

"Some of this is pretty old," Sullivan observed.

"I've got a date from ten years ago," I said, holding up a

strip of yellowed paper. I wrote down the nouns that I could read. A lot were medical terms that I didn't understand. I also noticed that the name Ray appeared several times.

"Most of these look like medical bills. Some are a lot older than others," Sullivan said. "I think the newer ones are for the late Mr. Schultz."

"Doesn't make a lot of sense to suddenly shred a bunch of old medical bills just before you hang yourself," Dad mumbled as he sorted through his own pile. "Mine look like phone records. What the heck was she covering up?"

"We'll keep working on them," Genie said, and Cara nodded.

"Some vacation," I said to Cara.

"I called Dr. Barnhill. I can stay on through tomorrow, but I have to head home tomorrow night. We've got animals boarding and Terry goes on vacation Wednesday. Besides, Ivy's going to want some attention and I need to pick up Alvin from his vacation with the doc."

"I'd apologize again, but you'd just hit me," I told her with a grin and gave her a light kiss.

"I can stay through tomorrow as well," Genie told Dad.

"That's right. The restaurant is closed on Monday," Dad said and took her hand.

"Is Dave okay with us staying a couple of extra days?" I asked, remembering that we were getting the rental through a friendship.

"I texted him and he said no problem," Dad answered.

With the domestic arrangements settled, we left Cara and Genie to their paper project and split up to conduct more interviews.

CHAPTER ELEVEN

I went back next door to the Leonards'. Bob's expression at the sight of me left no doubt that he wanted to slam the door in my face. I could see the internal battle raging behind his eyes before his better judgment prevailed.

"Come in," he said with reluctance. "I don't know what else we can tell you. Hell, you were here when we found the body."

"Is your wife around?"

"She's upstairs. I'll call her down."

"Don't. I'd rather talk with each of you individually," I said, receiving a cold stare in return.

"Whatever. Let's go downstairs."

I followed him down to his ground-floor man-cave, where he dropped into an over-stuffed leather chair that looked like it'd been around since the Reagan administration. I sat across from him in an old lawn chair.

"What do you know about Pauline Schultz?"

I'd been hoping for a reaction and I got one. Nothing dramatic, but his eyes widened and his pupils dilated. Bob couldn't keep himself from leaning forward a little.

"I know she killed herself," he said. I wasn't at all surprised that he already knew. Six hours was more than enough time for news to circle the island a dozen times.

"So how well did you know her?"

"Not well," he said with a shrug. "Seen her around."

"So you would recognize her? Knew her by name?" I pushed.

"Wouldn't have been able to tell you her name. But when I saw her in a store or something, I knew she lived here. In fact, Courtney had to pull out an issue of the local paper and show me a picture of her when we heard she'd hung herself." He said it with an openness that made me believe him. Still, he was hiding something.

"Can you think of anything that might connect you and Courtney with Mrs. Schultz?"

"Hey, what's this about? When I let you in, I thought you wanted to ask me some more questions about the body we found."

"We're looking into the possibility that the body and Mrs. Schultz's death might be related."

"You said her death? Is there a chance that it wasn't suicide?" Bob's demeanor had changed.

"In any death investigation we withhold judgment until the coroner has had a chance to do a full autopsy and issue a report," I explained.

"You saw her? What's your professional opinion?" Bob asked, giving me his full attention.

"I wouldn't want to speculate," I said, causing him to sit back in his chair and wave his hand dismissively.

"You must have an opinion."

"I asked you a question. Is there any other connection between your household and Mrs. Schultz's?" I pressed him.

He frowned. "We live on the same island. Bet we shop at some of the same stores, though we're certainly not in her income bracket. So those are connections, but anything more personal? No. Nothing."

"Do you know Ernest Wilkins?" I asked, moving on to the shooting.

"Are you kidding me? Wilkins owns half the island. We

bought our house from him. I don't think you could live out here and not know him. Hell, he's the president of the homeowners' association." Bob smiled for the first time since I'd come into the house. "Now, if you think we go to his house for dinner once a month, you're out of your mind. Wilkins and the Schultz woman, they could mingle. Us? Believe me, we don't get invitations to the Christmas parties."

"I hear your poor mouthing, but you're doing okay," I said, indicating the house. I made a mental note to run his credit. Maybe he was having money problems. Not that I could see how either death would have helped him financially.

"I do okay. We got our retirement. I sold our home up north for enough to buy this place. But there is a big difference between having the money to pay your bills and buying a Ferrari. And Ferraris don't park next to Chevy Suburbans." As though he needed to emphasize his working man creds, he added, "Crap, I need a beer."

He stood up and grabbed a bottle of beer from a small wet bar in the corner of the room. Holding it out to me, he asked, "You want one?"

"I'm good," I said. "Just a few more questions."

Bob plopped back down into his chair and looked at me.

"What about Blake Klein?"

"What about him?"

"You know him?"

"I just told you that we bought our house from Wilkins. We saw Wilkins once at the signing, but the rest of the time we dealt with Klein." Bob seemed to roll something over in his mind for a moment. "This about the shooting?"

"You heard about that?"

"The island tom-toms beat strong," he said, sounding like an extra in a 1950s Hollywood production.

"You like him?"

"No," Bob said flatly.

"Why not?"

"Because he was a pompous ass that wouldn't even take our last offer to Wilkins. All we wanted was an allowance in the contract for new appliances. We paid close to half a million dollars for this place and the jerk wouldn't even ask Wilkins to knock off five thousand dollars."

Bob was lightly tapping his beer bottle against the arm of the chair, clearly ready for me to leave. I was glad that I'd saved the reveal of Fowler's identity for a moment like this. If you give information in small payouts like a slot machine, it helps to keep the person you're questioning off guard and engaged in the interview.

"Did you know Claude Fowler?"

I saw something flicker in his eyes and his body tensed. The name clearly meant something to him.

"Might have heard of him," he said in an ass-covering move. "Who is he?" Bob tried to make his face look open and innocent.

"That's the man who was bobbing in the water off of your dock yesterday morning."

Bob's eyes narrowed. He hadn't known that. Maybe he'd suspected, but he hadn't known for sure.

"Really?" he asked, and I had to restrain myself from giving him a sarcastic answer.

"Where have you heard the name before?"

"I'm not sure I have. Fowler isn't that uncommon a name. What kind of work did he do?"

"Heating and air," I answered, watching him closely.

"Maybe that's it. We had to replace our unit last year. We went through the book getting estimates."

"You don't know him from anywhere else?"

"We told you we didn't recognize him yesterday. Now I'm telling you I don't know the name. Might have heard it, but I never met the guy. Look, I'm 'bout done with the questions," he said with heat, setting the beer bottle down on a side table with a *thunk* and standing up.

"I'd like to speak with Courtney," I said neutrally.

Bob gave me a cold look.

I followed him back up to the main floor and waited as he lumbered up the stairs. Five minutes later he made the trip back down. "She's not feeling well. Maybe tomorrow," he told me dismissively.

I hated to leave without talking to her, but I didn't have anything to pressure him with. As I walked back to our house, I rewound the interview in my mind. I hadn't gotten anything out of it but more suspicions. The name Fowler had meant something to Bob, though I was still pretty sure that the Leonards hadn't recognized Fowler when he was floating in the water.

Bob had seemed nervous at the idea that Schultz had been murdered, and not letting me talk to Courtney had been a power play. The Leonards would remain on my list of persons of interest, but there wasn't much else I could do with them right now. We'd need a better lever before we'd be able to pry more information out of them.

I found Dad and Mauser in the backyard of our house. Dad was on his cell phone, pacing back and forth while Mauser stood next to him, looking concerned. Dad was clearly worked up about something. *This can't be good*, I thought as I walked over to them. Mauser greeted me quickly then went back to staring at Dad and whining a little. Like me, the big goofus could tell that he was upset about something.

"I've got a friend that will take the case. Don't worry. I'll call him as soon as I hang up. Mrs. Peters, everything will be okay. Let me make a few calls. I'll let you know soon, I promise."

Dad ended the call and looked at me. There was so much anger in his face that I felt my stomach tighten. "That son of a bitch!" he said through clenched teeth.

"What's wrong?"

Dad held his hand up and stopped me. "I got to call Jay," he said, hitting a speed dial number on his phone.

Jay Moreno was one of the best defense lawyers in the Big Bend area. He was the go-to guy for cops who found themselves in legal problems, though the ones that were guilty shied away from him. Not because he wouldn't defend them, but because he had a way of letting them know that he didn't like defending guilty people. I'd asked him once what he said to the ones that he knew were guilty.

"Simple. I tell them that my job as a lawyer is to give them the best defense possible. But also that my job as a God-fearing man who believes in morals and the sanctity of the soul is to counsel them to take a sentence that's fair in order to pay their true debt to society. Funny, most of them decide they want another lawyer, which is just fine as wine with me."

Moreno was a renowned character in the courtroom, frequently sporting loud ties that you couldn't unsee. If Dad was calling the Jay Bird, then the shit had truly hit the fan.

"Jay, this is Ted. I've got an emergency." I knew that Jay's brain must have been going into overdrive hearing Dad say those words.

"I'm out on Pelican Island. I need you to head to the sheriff's office down here. There's a young man being questioned by Duncan and he needs some representation. His name is Jerome Martel. He's a good man, just a bit challenged. He doesn't have any family that anyone knows of. His landlord and friend is deeply concerned. Duncan came by and started questioning Jerome and, next thing the friend saw, he was being hauled off in handcuffs. Duncan told the friend that he wasn't under arrest, but that Jerome was being taken to the station for questioning." Dad stopped and listened for a minute. "This involves the murder of Jerome's boss. According to his friend Mrs. Peters, when she tried to stop him from taking Jerome, Duncan said that he'd found items belonging to the victim in Jerome's possession. He threatened her, saying that if she didn't back off and stay out of it, he'd haul her down to the jail too.

"No, I don't think she's exaggerating. Duncan has his wind up because Larry and I have been staying down here and stuck our noses into what he sees as his investigation. I don't know why he'd pick on Jerome. You know Duncan. He's pig-headed and now that he's got the bit in his teeth," Dad said, mixing his metaphors, "it's going to take a legal slap upside the head to get him to turn this man loose."

Dad gave him some more details about Fowler and the murder. "Thanks for coming down, Jay. I'm going to head up there and meet you."

Dad paused and I was sure that Moreno was finding a diplomatic way to talk Dad out of that crazy idea. "Are you sure? Okay, I'll wait for your call."

As soon as Dad hung up, he started grinding his teeth. From the look in his eye, I could tell that he wanted to punch a tree, but he'd been reining in his tendency to hit inanimate objects as he'd gotten older. "I can't believe he's that stupid and mean."

"He can't think that Jerome killed Fowler," I said.

Dad gave me a withering look. "Of course he can. The man's a jackass. And if Jay doesn't get there fast enough, Duncan is liable to get a confession out of Jerome."

Dad's reaction made me proud. He had an ego, but I knew that this was all about Jerome. Dad had a few presentations that he occasionally gave at law enforcement training seminars. One of them involved the importance of a quality interrogation and how to perform one. Nothing made him angrier than a confession coerced out of an innocent person. He'd lecture that getting a false confession was the equivalent of letting a bad guy go free. Confessions swayed juries and, once a person was convicted of a crime, all investigation stopped. Only in recent years, with the advancements involving DNA, had innocent men been given a second chance and real criminals brought to justice. Dad always ended his presentation by telling the people in attendance that locking up an innocent man made you guilty of two wrongs—persecuting an innocent man and letting a guilty man go free.

"There's nothing you can do right now but wait for Jay to bring the hammer down on Duncan," I told him.

The image of Jay hitting Duncan with a hammer brought a slight smile to Dad's face.

"The first forty-eight hours are the most important in an investigation," Dad said, looking at his watch. "We've got about twelve hours left. We need to crack this open."

I opened my mouth to say something encouraging, though I didn't really know what I could tell him. Dad knew as well as I did that solving a case like this depended on getting the right breaks, which was just a euphemism for luck. But I was saved from spouting out something stupid by the sound of Cara's voice.

"Hey guys, I'm going for pizza. What do you all want?" she asked brightly.

"Y'all don't want to go out?" I asked, a bit surprised. "It being the last night of vacation and all?"

"No, we've gotten a dozen pieces of the puzzle together and only have fifteen thousand to go. We'd hate to quit when we're so close," she joked.

"Kitchen sink for me," Dad said.

"Okay, one with everything. And…"

Cara flashed a smile at me that warmed my heart. Despite everything that had happened, I was grateful for the time we'd had together on the island. I took a moment to appreciate how beautiful she looked in the setting sun, then smiled at her and said, "You know I'll eat anything as long as it's called pizza."

A loud moan from the shade of a tree was Mauser's two cents on the pizza discussion.

"You aren't getting any pizza," Cara chided him. "That wouldn't be good for your tummy, which wouldn't be good for any of us." Mauser put his head down and gave her his best starving dog look.

"So an everything and an anything. You all are easy." Then she stopped and gave Dad a questioning look. "Is everything okay?"

"I'll walk with you to the car and tell you all about it," I said, taking her hand.

By the time we reached the car, I'd told her all I knew about Jerome being picked up by Duncan.

"Duncan would railroad him like that?" Cara asked, appalled. "I'm not naïve. I know that things like that have happened before, but…"

"A sheriff has a lot of power which can be used for good or ill."

"With great power comes great responsibility."

"And Dad takes his responsibilities very seriously. Even outside the bounds of his own jurisdiction," I said with a frown.

"Your Dad's pretty awesome."

"He's a little crazy, but I've never doubted that his goal is justice."

Cara put both her hands on my chest and I wrapped my arms around her. "You've got to solve this," she said.

"We'll do our best." I leaned in and started to kiss her when I heard Dad coming around the house with Mauser in tow.

"I'm putting him in the house, then I'm heading out to question one of Schultz's neighbors," Dad yelled to me. "You can come along."

"The great thing about pizza is you can heat it up in the microwave," Cara said and broke away from me. "I'd better go get it so I can come back and help Genie with our art project."

She had just driven off when Dad came back out of the house. "You coming?" he asked, climbing into his truck.

CHAPTER TWELVE

"Who are we going to see?" I asked Dad.

"Molly Cortez. Sally said that she'd gone on a couple of cruises with Pauline Schultz. From what everyone's told Sally, Mrs. Cortez is as close to a best friend as Schultz had."

"Sally called you?"

"No, I checked in with her while you were escorting your girlfriend to the car," he said, sounding annoyed that I was questioning how he'd come by his information.

Molly Cortez lived just two doors down from Pauline Schultz. When she answered the door, she looked frail and lost.

"Who are you again?" she asked after Dad had rushed through the introductions. We showed her our badges and explained that we were out of our jurisdiction, but were helping local law enforcement with the investigation into Pauline Schultz's death.

She opened the door wide and, walking with a slight stoop, escorted us into a beautiful living room. The view out over the Gulf was amazing as the sky turned purple and orange in the fading sunlight.

Mrs. Cortez eased herself down onto the couch. "I can't believe that Pauline killed herself. I don't have that many friends left. I'm eighty-two," she said, giving us a sad smile. I guessed that, at her age, loss became as much about you as it did the person who'd died.

"How long have you known Mrs. Schultz?" Dad asked. He was leaning forward with a sympathetic expression on his face that he reserved for the elderly. I could remember how he'd taken care of his mother in her last years. He'd stop by her house whenever he finished his shift or during his meal breaks to check on her. He'd never once complained or seemed to mind the extra responsibility.

"Since Pauline and her husband moved here. Five years ago, something like that. But we didn't really become friends until her husband passed away. He'd been sick. Cancer or something horrible like that. The last six months she was spending all her time taking care of him."

"But you all got to know each other after he died?" Dad prompted.

"Yes, I'd gone over with a double chocolate layer cake I baked a day or two after I'd heard that her husband had passed. Well, she invited me in for coffee. We talked for a while and I told her how, after my first husband Hugh had passed, I went on a cruise to just clear my mind. Get a fresh perspective on the world. Well, she said that sounded like a wonderful idea. I told her I had some brochures I'd bring her. I did just that the next day. We talked some more and decided that we'd go together on a Caribbean cruise. Pauline was a lot of fun and a good traveling companion. We took two, no, three more trips after that."

"Had you seen her much in the last couple of weeks?" I asked.

"We'd go to lunch every Wednesday and do some shopping. One of the things I liked about her was that she never cancelled on me. I hate it when people make dates and then cancel all the time. Unreliable. Not Pauline. If she said she was going to do something, she did it." I could see the veil of loss come down across Molly's face.

"So you all went to lunch this past Wednesday?" Dad

encouraged.

"Oh, yes, we drove into Apalachicola, had lunch and did a little shopping."

"Did she seem different?" Dad asked.

"What do you mean by different?" Molly asked.

I knew that Dad wanted to be careful not to give her any ideas. It was too easy to suggest that someone was acting a certain way to the point that the person being interviewed began to remember it that way, even if that wasn't the case at all.

"Anything out of the ordinary. Did she say anything that surprised you or act in some way that wasn't what you expected?"

"Let me think. I was really enjoying the little trip. It was cloudy and a bit rainy, so it wasn't too hot. We had a really nice time. No. I'd say she was just like she always was."

"And how was that? What was she normally like?"

"Good, happy. She had a great smile. Pauline would always try and trick me when the bill came. We had a deal where we alternated who paid for lunch. When it was my turn she'd always try to convince me that it was hers. We'd go back and forth and then she'd finally let me pay. I have plenty of money. Manuel left me quite well off and she knew that. It was just a game." More dark clouds crossed her face.

"Can you think of any reason that she might have wanted to take her own life?" Dad asked.

"No. I..." Molly got a faraway look in her eyes.

"What?"

"She had her share of tragedy in her life. Her first husband died after a long illness and then Ray went in almost the same way. It must have been hard. At least when my Hugh died, it was quick. He was out mowing our lawn, just like he did every Saturday in the summer. I went out to take him a beer, and he was just lying there next to the mower. They said it was a massive heart attack. I know that if a loved one is sick they say you have time to prepare for their passing, but I think it's better when they go fast. When I think of Hugh, it's always of the good times. There really weren't any bad ones. Now Manuel, he was a lot older than me, so when he went it wasn't a surprise. I miss him. He was very kind to me. Never refused me a thing." Molly looked up at us. "I'm sorry for the trip down memory lane. Seems that's all I can do these days. Pauline was such a good listener. I know I repeat myself, but she never seemed bothered by me telling her the same stories."

"So you think the deaths of her husbands could have contributed to her wanting to take her own life?" Dad didn't sound convinced. I had to admit it was hard to believe that she'd suddenly be overwhelmed by grief from two losses that had taken place years ago.

"Well, she did have the issue with her son," Molly said without elaborating.

"What was that?" I pushed.

"He just didn't seem to care about her. I didn't even know she had a son until a year ago. I was helping her clean out her closet. She was going to get one of those girls who come in and design your closet for you, so we had to take everything out. When I was emptying a drawer, I came across a framed picture of Pauline with a young man. It was one of those graduation photos. Him in a gown and a… What do you call it? …A mortarboard. Molly had her arm around him. Both with these big smiles. I said, 'Who is this?' At first, I didn't think Pauline was going to tell me. She just stared at the picture with this really, really sad expression on her face. I felt like I'd ruined things by asking her, because she'd been in a great mood while we were cleaning out the closet. Then I'd gone and upset her. But after a few moments she looked up at me and said, 'That's my son.' Well, my heart just sank. From the way she looked and the way she sounded, I thought he'd died. I thought how awful it was to have faced three deaths. I wasn't going to ask any more questions, so it surprised me when she said that he didn't want to be in her life anymore. Can you beat that? I've known families to get in squabbles, but to just walk out of your mother's life?"

"Did you ask her why?"

"No. But she did say that he blamed her for his father's death. I mean, the man had cancer or something. How could he blame his mother for that?" Molly sounded truly appalled. "Now what's he going to do? There's no making it up now. Life is too short for that bullshit. Pardon my French."

I suddenly wanted to be there when Sullivan met with this son. Clearly there was a story here. Anything that could drive a wedge that deep into a family might be powerful enough to cause other repercussions.

"Have you ever seen this man?" Dad showed her Fowler's driver's license photo.

"I need my glasses," she said, putting on the pair she wore around her neck. "No. I don't think so."

"Did Mrs. Schultz ever mention a man named Claude Fowler?" I asked.

She mulled the name over for a moment. "No. Is that him in the picture? Wait, was he the man that was found floating in the water yesterday?"

With no reason not to tell her, we affirmed both of her questions.

"I heard about that. Tex who lives next door, his grandson works with the ambulance folks and helped pull the body out of the water. Tex is always telling me what that grandson is doing. Sometimes it's pretty awful. Accidents and everything." Molly waved her hand and made a face as though she was smelling a bad odor, but I suspected that she liked hearing the gruesome stories.

We stayed awhile longer and listened to Molly's reminiscences of the trips she had taken with Pauline. By the time it was dark, Molly was losing her energy. We thanked her and told her we'd keep her posted on the investigation.

Dad was texting Jay Moreno before we even got back in the truck. He received an answer as he started to pull out of the driveway. "Read it," he told me.

"Says: *No good news. They have him, but say he's agreed to talk without a lawyer. He's legally an adult, so there isn't much I can do. From the smartass smirk on the investigator's face, I'd say they're getting what they want."*

Dad launched into a tirade of curse words, punctuated by a good pounding on the steering wheel. It had been a long time since I'd seen him this upset. *Not good*, I thought.

"You get real used to living in a world were you have some control," he said in a cold, tight tone. "So help me..."

"We need to talk to Pauline's son," I said, trying to distract him.

"Call Sullivan and find out when the son is arriving."

I didn't point out to him that Sullivan had said the man was flying in this evening and we probably wouldn't get to talk to him until tomorrow. It was already eight-thirty.

I got Sullivan on the phone. He was with Dr. Thomlinson, who he'd managed to talk into doing Pauline's autopsy. Seemed Thomlinson had dreams of being a full-time forensic pathologist and the recent spate of odd deaths had intrigued him. I filled Sullivan in on how Duncan had dragged Jerome in for questioning.

"Asshole," was Sullivan's one-word response. Then he went on to tell me that the son, Owen Lampert, was flying into the airport in Panama City, but that he didn't know his exact arrival time.

I got through to the airport just as we pulled into our driveway. After a few assurances that I was who I was, I got an agent who told me that Lampert's flight was scheduled to arrive at ten-thirty.

"Ten-thirty," Dad said thoughtfully, and I knew exactly what was going through his head.

"I'm starving," I said, not caring one bit that I must have sounded like a five-year-old.

"Fine. We'll go in, get some food and then head out to meet this Lampert character at the airport. Save him a car rental." From Dad's tone, I knew that Lampert wasn't going to have a choice about accepting a ride from us.

"This smells fantastic," I said a few minutes later, when I

finally fell into a chair holding a plate covered with three slices of Italian goodness.

Dad came over with his own plate. "Called Sullivan and told him we were going to pick up Lampert," he said, tearing into a slice.

"Any word on Jerome?" Cara asked.

I told her the little bit we knew while Dad put his pizza down and texted Jay for another update. Then he went back to shoveling food into his mouth. I'd seen him like this hundreds of times when I was growing up. When he was working a case he had a tenacity that was unrelenting. The few cases that he wasn't able to solve took their toll. He'd given a year of his life to the Swamp Hacker case over fifteen years ago, and it had driven him crazy when the case was declared cold and he was pulled off of the investigation. It had taken him almost another year to let it go.

His phone buzzed with an answer from the lawyer. Dad read it and we could all see his face flush.

"They still have Jerome in an interrogation room. Six hours so far," Dad said through clenched teeth. "Jay's trying to get a judge to grant him access on the basis of diminished capacity."

"That's awful," Genie said. "When I think about Jimmy being in a situation like that, it's terrifying."

"There are unscrupulous cops who will take advantage of someone with fewer resources," Dad said, reaching out and taking her hand. His pizza was long gone. "I'm going to do everything I can for Jerome."

"I know that," Genie said to him with an affection that told me how much trust and love was growing between them. It had weirded me out a bit when Dad first started dating a woman who'd been my babysitter and known my mother, but now I could see all the good that was coming from them spending time together. Cara had noticed it too. She reached over and took my hand, giving it an affectionate squeeze.

With a little time to kill before we had to leave for the

airport, Dad and I helped Genie and Cara with their puzzle. Cara had stopped at a drug store when she went for the pizza and bought some supplies. They were gluing some of the strips onto pieces of paper, and she'd found translucent sheets for the pieces with words printed on both sides. Our efforts were not aided by Mauser. Irritated that we'd managed to ignore the appeal of his big brown eyes all during dinner, he tried to crawl under the table and almost knocked it over.

"You don't fit, you big lummox. How many times do we have to tell you?" I scolded him. My insults never seemed to have any effect on his ego.

"I'll go get him a pig's ear," Dad said indulgently.

I looked at all the scraps of paper and realized it was a good thing that Ivy wasn't here to help. Having a cat pounce on all the piles was the last thing we'd need.

"I don't understand," I said, looking over some of the completed work. "I mean, I know what all of this is. Bills, prescriptions, and then there are these receipts for work done on her house. But why would she feel compelled to shred all of this?"

"Maybe it's a red herring," Dad said apologetically. I knew that he didn't want to imply that Genie and Cara were wasting their time, but you always had to consider that what looked like a great clue wasn't.

"Maybe it's a red herring placed there by someone who murdered her and wanted it to look like she'd done all of this in preparation for a suicide," I suggested.

"Maybe," Dad said uncertainly. "My gut says that this means something, though."

"I certainly hope so," Genie said with a smile, peering at him over the top of her reading glasses.

CHAPTER THIRTEEN

I watched Dad as he drove us to the airport, speeding a little too fast and his eyes focused on a point beyond the headlights.

"What are you going to do if he doesn't want to ride with us?" I asked.

"Knocking him in the head and throwing him in the back of the truck would defeat the purpose. I want to learn what he knows." I wasn't sure if he was kidding or not. "We'll just have to play it by ear. The death of his mother, the trip here... Hopefully all of that will put him in the mood to talk. We'll go in being as non-confrontational as possible. Tell him that the police chief sent us and see where it goes."

"So we're going to pretend that this is a courtesy service?" I kidded him.

"We'll let him believe whatever he wants."

"Don't you think he's going to wonder why your truck has Adams County Sheriff decals all over it?"

"It's late. It's dark. We'll see what he notices and what he doesn't."

"I never knew you were so sneaky."

"Ha, you should have seen me and Pat Weber when we were young bucks. We used to pull off some very creative sting operations."

Weber had been one of Dad's first partners and best friends in the department. Sadly, Weber had died in a single car accident twelve years ago. Dad had persistently denied that it was a suicide, but the highway patrol and the lead Adams County investigator had determined that the accident had all the hallmarks of a person using their car to kill themself. The sad fact is that suicide rates for law enforcement officers are very high. Just because you don't see any evidence that a person is suicidal doesn't mean they aren't. Of course, this could apply to Mrs. Schultz as much as it did to Weber.

"I can see you two getting into trouble."

"One time we knew, I mean *knew*, that this guy—Marvin was his name—was stealing lawnmowers. But he had some pipeline set up where they were out of our county so fast that we couldn't catch him with them. So, there was this guy who lived on a route that Marvin took to buy cigarettes every day, and we talked him into helping us set a trap. We cleaned up a zero-turn mower. It had something terminal wrong with it, so the repair guy didn't mind us taking it. We put the mower at just the right place in this guy's garage where Marvin couldn't help but see it, yet it didn't look like a hunk of cheese in a mousetrap either. Well, we took one of those bank dye packs and hooked it up to the battery under the seat of the mower. When Marvin went to start the mower, that pack exploded and his legs were covered in bright red dye." Dad started to laugh so hard that I thought he was going to run us off the road.

"What?" I asked as he coughed and tried to get his composure back. "It's a funny story, but not *that* funny."

"No, the funny part is that, when Marvin looked down and saw his legs were all red, he thought they'd been torn apart by the explosion. He was screaming for an ambulance when we got there," Dad said, still chuckling.

"You have a very strange sense of humor," I said, trying not to laugh.

We met Owen Lampert at baggage claim. He was of medium height with black hair and his mother's angular face and prominent chin.

"Who are you again?" he asked.

Dad took out his badge and gave him more of an explanation than he'd originally planned to. Owen appeared to be naturally suspicious.

"I could have just called an Uber," he said, sounding tired.

"We'll save you the hundred bucks," I said.

He looked over at me and, for a second, I thought he was going to ask me to show my badge as well. But then a resigned look came over his face. "Fine. Whatever. I just want to get all of this over with," he said, sounding quite sincere.

I put his suitcase in the back of the truck while he kept his carryon with him. Dad told him to sit up front while I took the jump seat in the extended cab. There was a cage installed, so I had Plexiglas separating me from the front of the truck. I don't think Dad had ever had a prisoner in the back, but I guess he had to be prepared.

I hunched forward with my head close to the Plexiglas so I could hear their conversation over the noise of the truck. I only hoped that Dad wouldn't need to slam on the brakes at any point.

"Sorry about your mother," Dad said once we were moving.

Owen stared out the windshield "Don't be. Not for my sake."

"Y'all didn't get along?"

"That's an understatement."

"We're trying to understand her death. I'm hoping you can help us."

"I couldn't care less why or how she died," Owen said bluntly.

"That's a little harsh."

111

"You can think that," Owen said, still not turning to look at Dad and just staring out the windshield at the darkness.

"Everyone deserves to have justice."

"You don't know what the hell you're talking about. Can we just drop it?"

I could see Dad purse his lips. It irritated him when someone wouldn't go even a little bit out of their way to help with an investigation. The fact that this was the man's mother made it even more irritating.

"I don't know what happened between you and your mother, but if there's a chance that someone killed her, then you need to help us. If it's suicide, fine. But at this point we don't know that, which means there could be a killer out there," Dad said.

"'I am become death, the destroyer of worlds,'" Owen said.

"That's from one of the guys that made the first atomic bomb," Dad said.

"Robert Oppenheimer."

"Yeah, that's right. What kind of work do you do?" Dad asked, choosing a different conversational direction to get the son talking.

"I'm a history professor."

"A full professor?"

"Actually, yeah."

"Wow, you must have written some books or know how to schmooze." Dad laughed. It was pure theatre, nothing like his guffaws at the hapless Marvin.

"A little of both," Owen admitted. He turned his head and looked at Dad as he answered. *Houston, we have contact,* I thought.

"What's your area of expertise?"

"The American Century."

"Nice. Both World Wars, the Cold War, John, Bobby and Martin. Lots of death and destruction."

"I used that quote as the title for my first book, an overview of the century. *Destroyer of Worlds.*" Owen sounded wistful.

"Sell well?"

"Ha, nobody cares about history anymore. They're all too self-involved. Way too invested in their own petty agendas. My publisher told me that if it was written from a left- or right-wing perspective, then he could guarantee me ten times the revenue."

"I hear that," Dad said sympathetically. "I'm in the history business myself." I was curious to see where Dad was going with this.

"I thought you were the sheriff of some other county, which, honestly, I don't get why you're looking into my… Her death."

"Investigating crimes is writing history. We do it right and the truth goes down in the record. We screw it up or just can't get enough information and it leaves a gap in history. It's a hole that others will try and fill, but with each minute that passes, it gets harder and harder to get to the truth." Dad stopped, letting the implications sink in.

"You think I'm standing in your way?" Owen asked. He was staring at Dad's face illuminated by the dash lights.

"Aren't you?"

"Anything I could tell you would be old news. I haven't seen my mother in well over a decade."

"Not since your father died?"

"Yep." Owen turned back to the windshield and the blackness beyond the headlights.

Dad tried several more ploys before giving up and driving the last ten miles in silence. Owen had insisted on being taken to Mrs. Schultz's house. Her next door neighbor, Mr. Henderson, met us and opened up the house. There was a minor kerfuffle when none of us knew the security code. Sally had reset it when we'd left that afternoon. A call to Sullivan helped to convince the security company that we were legit.

However, the issue with the alarm provided Dad and me with an excuse to follow Owen into the house.

"Look, it's been a long trip. I had to run to catch my connection in Atlanta."

"You were lucky to get down here so fast," Dad said.

"What does that mean?"

"Nothing. You're just lucky it wasn't a holiday or something. Hard enough to get a flight in here as it is."

"I wanted to get things cleared up." Owen looked around, unsure how to get us out of the house. I knew that Dad would drag his feet as much as possible until he got something out of Owen that we could use.

"Why don't we walk through the house with you?" Dad suggested.

"That's not necessary," Owen said firmly.

"We still don't know if your mother killed herself or was murdered. I think the safest thing would be for us to walk through the house and make sure that there's no one lurking in a closet."

"The alarm was set," Owen insisted.

"Humor me."

"We walk through and then you leave?"

"Sure," Dad said in a tone that left plenty of wiggle room. I felt like a bystander in a chess match.

We started downstairs in the garage. There was an almost-new red BMW parked in the immaculate space. It looked more like a white room in a laboratory than a garage. There were no tools to be found, only a few beach items on a shelf. Clearly Pauline Schultz was not a DIY kind of woman. We didn't find any bogeymen either.

On the second level we went through the kitchen and the large living/dining space. Walking by a bookshelf, Owen suddenly stopped. As though he was being controlled like a marionette, his hand reached out and took a book off of the shelf. The title was *Destroyer of Worlds: America in the 20th Century*. The book had been well read. Owen flipped through the pages and saw numerous notes in the margins. I caught a few words such as *clever*, *perfect* and *smart*. His hand was shaking as he put the book back on the shelf next to several other books that appeared equally well read. The author of those was also the eminent Dr. Owen Lampert.

As we walked through the rest of the house, Owen seemed to be in a daze. We came back to the living room and he just stood there for a while, not acknowledging us. Dad didn't say or do anything, letting the silence and awkwardness grow.

After what must have been ten minutes of watching Owen stare out the large plate glass windows at the night, he turned to Dad and, in a very small voice, said, "I'll answer some of your questions."

"I appreciate that. Why don't we sit down?" I didn't know if Dad suggested this to encourage Owen to answer more questions or because his hip was bothering him. While we had been waiting for Owen to decide what to do, I'd noticed him shifting his weight back and forth. Growing old isn't for sissies.

Dad and I sat on the couch while Owen sat across from us in a flowery chair. He looked out of place.

"Let's start with why you and your mother weren't on good terms."

"Ha, start with the hardest first. I don't…" I thought Dad might have made a mistake. For a moment it looked like Owen was going to stand up and ask us to leave. But after another protracted pause, he went on, "I guess it doesn't matter anymore. I made her a promise twelve years ago when my father died not to tell anyone what I knew. I think that promise died with her. If nothing else, at this point, it'll be good to get it off my chest." He stopped again. The man had a thing for dramatic pauses.

"Go on." Dad apparently thought he could risk pushing Owen a little.

"All right, she killed my father." Another one of his damned dramatic pauses. Maybe his students liked them.

"Didn't your father die of cancer or something?"

"He had lymphoma. He'd gone into remission once, but the cancer came back."

"So…"

"He was in a lot of pain. My father asked us to help him commit suicide. I refused. He'd gone into remission before. It was just a rough patch. He was feeling down and she took advantage of that," Owen said, his voice shaking with emotion.

"Owen, if the man was that ill… I mean, technically, yes, she did commit murder, but if you love someone and you have to watch them lying there…"

I knew Dad was thinking of my mother. She'd suffered an aneurysm and had gone fairly fast, but there had still been the days in intensive care and the decision to remove life support. I remembered how hard it was for Dad to give that final order, even though it was the right thing to do.

"There are quality of life decisions that are hard to make," I finished for him.

"You don't understand. She didn't love him."

"Why do you say that?"

"Two years before my father got cancer, I'd just gone off to college. I came home one Thursday, a day earlier than she expected me. When I pulled into the driveway there was a big SUV parked there. I just figured some friend was visiting, so I went in the rear entrance. Mom hadn't bothered to close the bedroom door. She was sprawled out like a… He was on top of her… Moving." Owen's voice held a creepy anger. I felt like I was listening to Norman Bates.

"Understandably disturbing," Dad said. "But do you know for sure that she helped your dad end his own life?"

"Yes. He told me she was going to do it. I wanted to tell him about finding her entangled on their bed with another man, but I couldn't do it. I just couldn't tell him. Maybe if I had, he would have kicked her out. Maybe he'd have gone back for more treatment and into remission."

"You can't think like that," Dad said, shaking his head. "You made the right decision not telling him about the other man. Did your mom know that you'd seen her?"

"I think she suspected. I snuck out of the house, but

116

when I came back later she gave me a funny look. And she said some stuff later that made me feel like she knew I knew."

"How did your dad die?"

"Morphine overdose. I think she probably put a bag over his head too. When he was trying to talk me into it, that's how he said it was done."

"Did you tell the police?"

"No. I'd promised Dad. Later I told her that I'd never tell, but that I didn't want anything more to do with her. Four years later, she married the other guy."

"You never met him?"

"No, I never saw her after Dad's funeral."

"You've suffered for their sins," Dad said.

"Her sins," Owen clarified.

"Maybe. But the odds are you don't know the whole story."

"I know enough."

"Fine, but now you're only hurting yourself. They're all past caring." Dad was giving Owen his best bedside manner.

"Odd that her second husband died in almost the same way and this time she came out of it with a lot more money." The words came rushing out of Owen. Clearly he'd kept these ideas bottled up for years.

"You think she might have killed her second husband?" Dad asked the obvious.

"When I heard that he'd died, I found the obituary. It said he died quietly in his sleep after a protracted illness. Exactly the same thing it said when my dad died."

"It's not impossible for someone to marry two people who contract terminal illnesses," I said reasonably.

"Maybe."

"Look, we'll check it out. That's kind of our job," Dad said. I knew where he was going. I'd been there myself. After you'd gotten a witness all churned up and it was time for you to leave, you tried to pour some oil on the water before you left the person alone for the night.

"Do it. I want to know. I think I deserve to know if she was some kind of black widow or something."

"Don't worry. We'll keep you in the loop. We also need you to keep your eyes peeled. Especially as you go through your mother's things. If you see anything that seems out of place or that, in your judgment, may shed light on her death or the deaths of her husbands, call me." Dad took out his card, flipped it over and wrote my personal cell number on it.

I was somewhere between too wired to sleep and too sleepy to stay awake as we drove back to the house.

"I can't believe you gave him my phone number," I said grumpily.

"I need to keep my private cell number close to my vest," Dad said dismissively.

"Normally I wouldn't mind, but that guy is definitely getting close to the line of psychologically damaged goods."

"He'll be okay. This is going to help him clear the pipes. The guy's been holding a lot of crap inside for years."

"I think we ought to make sure he has an alibi for the death of his mother."

"That we can agree on. Though I think Owen as a suspect is a long shot."

"Weirdo with mother issues isn't that long of a shot. He's been haunted by the events surrounding his mother's infidelity and his father's assisted suicide for years. He finds out a couple of years ago that it looks like she offed another one, so he starts stalking her. She hires a private eye because she catches wind of her stalker, probably doesn't realize it's her son. Fowler gets too close, Norman kills him. Hey, that actually happened in the movie. It would explain how he got down here so quick..."

"Yeah, then how did he get back to New York quick enough to turn around and be on the flight this evening, Sherlock? Those records are easily checked," Dad said as he pulled into our driveway.

"I'll check them," I told him.

"You need to get some sleep."

"I plan on it."

Before we got out of the car, Dad's phone buzzed. I looked at the clock. Nothing good comes from a phone call or text after one o'clock in the morning.

"Damn it! Jay says they've booked Jerome on murder charges. One of the deputies told Jay they have a signed confession." Dad hit the steering wheel. The poor truck was taking quite the beating this weekend.

Cara and Genie were still up, drinking wine on the balcony, when we came in. They must have seen the looks on our faces because they both came over and offered big hugs. Dad gave them the CliffsNotes version of the night's events, leaving out some of the cuss words.

"I'll text Sullivan and let him know what's going on," Dad said before walking off toward their bedroom, leaning just a little on Genie.

I got a quick shower and Cara and I fell into bed. Between nightmares where crazed killers were stabbing their mothers and Cara's wine-induced snoring, I had a restless night. I was finally sound asleep when Dad knocked on the door.

CHAPTER FOURTEEN

I answered the door in my boxers.

"We need to get moving," Dad told me.

"What's up?" I looked at my watch, which reported that it was only eight o'clock. By my best calculation, I couldn't have gotten more than six hours of sleep, and it was probably closer to five.

"Sullivan and Jay are downstairs. Get dressed and come on down."

Dad's tone left no room for argument. I wanted to make a joke or give him a hard time, but I didn't have the heart. I knew why he was cracking the whip. I thought about Jerome sitting in jail and turned around, hunting for a clean pair of pants. I didn't have any luck, settling for a pair that I'd only worn once. I hadn't planned on my vacation running past Sunday.

"I'm up," Cara said unconvincingly. She looked like a particularly lethargic zombie when she reached out and grabbed my hand. I leaned over to kiss her, then headed downstairs, passing Mauser on the landing. He'd apparently decided there was too much going on downstairs and that retreat was in order if he was going to get his full twelve hours of sleep. I tried not to be too envious.

Genie was making coffee and setting out fresh honey buns that Sullivan had picked up from a local bakery. Sally sat at the dining room table, drinking a large cup of brew and looking as hung-over as I felt. I saw Sullivan and Jay together on the couch, deep in discussion. Good mornings were exchanged all around.

"It's a party," I said, trying to sound upbeat but failing.

Dad gave me a look, but kept his *You look like hell* to himself.

A cup of coffee and two honey buns later, I was feeling more alive.

"Come over here," Dad called to me. He'd joined the chief and the lawyer in the living room. "I filled them in on Owen's story."

"It really looks like Schultz was a suicide," Sullivan reported. "Thomlinson can't say for sure until the toxicology comes back, but he did say that there were no signs of anything out of the ordinary. He promised to run the widest toxicology screening the county could afford, but that will take more time. I think we have to move forward with this one in the suicide column until there is hard evidence to the contrary."

"Which begs the question, why? And why now? What compelled her to kill herself yesterday morning?" I asked, feeling a sense of anger and urgency rising in me. Maybe it was just a lack of sleep or the need to get an innocent man out of jail.

"Those are the right questions," Dad said. "She'd hired Fowler. Fowler was killed, so she committed suicide. Was that all cause and effect? What we're missing are the connecting motivating factors that drive that narrative."

"My client—," Jay started, then admitted, "Actually, he isn't technically my client yet since I've been denied access to him."

"How can they do that?" Sally asked.

"He's of age and hasn't asked for a lawyer. A man in jail isn't required to hire a lawyer. When he's arraigned the judge will assign him a public defender if he doesn't have a lawyer. When that happens, I'm sure that the public defender will be more than glad to let me talk to Jerome."

"When will he be arraigned?" Genie asked from the kitchen.

"This afternoon. The court in this county has a strange schedule. Most counties handle their weekend pickups first thing Monday morning. But the story here is that, back in the fifties, they had a couple of judges that either liked to drink heavily on the weekends or go duck hunting. Maybe both. Either way, they didn't like getting to court first thing on Monday morning. So court starts at noon on Mondays."

"What about the shooting?" I said. "That has never fit with any of our narratives."

"An outlier?" Dad suggested.

"I don't like it," I argued.

"If the shots had come from the water, I might buy that it was a random event. People get crazy when they get in a boat and have a few drinks. But from the street, here on the island, I don't accept it. The person who fired those shots had a motive," Sullivan said.

"Maybe they did, but the motive doesn't have anything to do with our dead body or the suicide investigation," Sally offered.

"First off, are we all on board that the murder and the suicide are connected?" Dad asked to general head nodding. "Okay, so the question on the floor is if the shooting is part of the same series of events. My thoughts are that there's a tie-in. Maybe a tenuous one, but there is something that links all of them together. We know that Schultz didn't fire those shots, and Fowler certainly didn't since he was already dead. So the question is, did the person who murdered Fowler try to kill Blake Klein?"

"I think we can be sure that the shots were either fired at random or were intended for Klein. Their path was pretty clear. I can see why, in the heat of the moment, Wilkins thought they might have been meant for him, but..." I let the thought hang in the air.

"I agree," Sullivan nodded. "Though I would think that Wilkins would have more enemies than Klein. He's just his flunky."

"A well paid flunky," Dad said.

"And as we learned from Bob Leonard, Klein is the one who plays hardball on behalf of Wilkins. Klein is the person most people interact with," I pointed out.

"True, that," Sally chimed in.

"And don't forget that he lied about it. The grapefruit is proof of that," I said, trying to sound like Hercule Poirot.

"Grapefruit?" Jay asked, no doubt already imagining a jury's reaction as he presented them with a grapefruit as evidence. We explained the significance of the citrus and he nodded.

"I'll do a thorough background on Klein," Sally offered.

"And we'll go talk to him," Dad said, nodding toward me. I was a little puzzled as to how we'd become inseparable partners. After I'd hit puberty, almost everything we'd tried to do together had turned into an awkward experience that we'd both felt was best forgotten. But I was willing to give the buddy thing a shot.

"I did find some security camera footage that I can review," Sally said. "Several neighbors near the shooting and Mrs. Schultz's house had cameras on their driveways which show parts of the street. Unfortunately, there aren't any on the front of Schultz's house or Klein's. Wilkins has a camera, but it doesn't point in the right direction."

"Do you mind going through that and making notes on cars approaching the scenes an hour before and after?" Dad asked.

"No, my husband will be thrilled. He's been stuck with rug rat duty. I can babysit while I watch the videos. I'll tell the kids it's a reality show and they'll sit there all day," Sally said with a smile. "I've already got about half the footage. And I can do the background on Klein from the house too."

"After what you told us about your interview with the

Leonards, I want to dig into their backgrounds a little deeper," Sullivan said.

"Good idea. Run a credit check on them too," Dad suggested.

"I've also got a couple leads on boat rental places that might have recognized the picture of Fowler that Sally sent to them. I'll follow up on that."

We spent a few more minutes discussing strategy before going our separate ways and promising to keep each other updated. It was a very odd little task force we'd put together.

Dad and I arrived at Blake Klein's house just in time to see him backing out of the driveway. Dad pulled his truck in behind him, blocking Klein's access to the street.

"This is perfect," Dad said. "I wanted to push his buttons. Let's see how he reacts to this." He got out of the truck and walked over to Klein, who was already storming forward to confront him.

"I'm really sorry to bother you, but we need to ask you a few more questions about the shooting." Dad didn't sound sorry at all.

"Can't right now. I've got a meeting in Panama City in an hour, so if you'll move your truck? I'll call you when I have time." Klein put on a smile, but I could tell that he wasn't happy.

I chose that moment to get out of the truck, making it clear that we weren't planning on getting out of his way anytime soon. I swear I could see his blood pressure start to spike.

"With two people dead and a shooter on the loose, we really don't have time to wait for you to find time to meet with us," Dad said.

"Come on, guys. Seriously, this is an important meeting." Klein still thought he had a chance of pleading to our better natures.

"What is the meeting about?" Dad asked, putting Klein in the awkward position of either telling us his business or refusing to tell us, which would only click this up a notch on the confrontation scale.

"It's important, but it doesn't have anything to do with what's been happening on the island." Klein tried a workaround.

"How do you know that?" Dad said.

"Because I didn't have anything to do with any of it and the meeting is personal," Klein said in frustration.

I'd moved closer to his car. On the passenger seat was a hat and a pair of golf gloves. "Golf game?" I asked innocently.

Klein looked at me, lips thin and eyes narrowed. "Yes, we're going to play golf, but we're also working on a real estate development deal. It's a meeting!" This last bit was said with some heat.

"I don't understand why you aren't more interested in catching the person who shot at you."

Dad had chosen just the right moment to toss this out. Confusion flashed across Klein's face. He had to make the switch from a conversation about the merits of a golf game to defending his attitude about something he'd formerly denied even happened.

"No one shot at me," he said, not sounding at all convincing as his voice broke like a twelve-year-old lying to his parents.

"We know someone shot at you," Dad said. A statement, not a question.

"I told you. I was upstairs when the shots were fired."

"No, you said you didn't hear the shots. How would you know when they were fired if you didn't hear them?" Dad asked, raising his eyebrows.

Klein opened and closed his mouth several times as he attempted to come up with an answer.

"Fine!" he shouted angrily and took out his phone, punching a number.

"Steve! Hey, I've got to reschedule our game. No, I'm fine. Had a suicide on the island and some other issues come up over the weekend and the police need some information from me." All of this was said with the honey-sweet tones of someone who doesn't have a problem in the world. "Sure, sounds great. I'll text you some possible times."

He hung up and gave us a hard look. "Hope you're happy," he told us childishly. "Let's go inside."

We followed him back up to the room where we'd talked before.

"What do you want to know?"

"We can start off with why you lied about the shooting," Dad said.

Klein sighed dramatically. "I didn't want to go into my personal problems. I don't think the person was trying to kill me."

"Generally, when someone shoots at you it's a safe assumption that they're trying to kill you," Dad said sternly.

"I think this had more to do with intimidation than murder."

"Why don't you let us be the judge of that. Who shot at you and why?"

"I didn't actually see them. But if it's who I think it was, it has to do with an affair I was having. Honestly, it could be one of two people."

"Let me guess. The husband or the wife?"

"Yes. I've been seeing this woman for a couple of months. She's got some... issues, so I broke it off. That was Friday night."

"So what makes you think she might have been shooting at you?"

"I told her I didn't want to see her anymore. She'd gotten very clingy and had threatened to hurt herself if I stopped seeing her."

"But you went ahead and told her you were breaking it off?"

"I wasn't going to submit to her emotional blackmail, so what choice did I have? Her last words to me Friday night were that I was going to be sorry. So, Saturday afternoon, I pull into my driveway, get my groceries out of the back and, next thing I know, I'm dodging bullets."

"But you didn't call the police."

"Look, if she wanted to kill me she could have come up to me in the carport and shot me at point-blank range. Why stand out in the street and lob a few rounds in my direction? I wanted time to figure this out on my own."

"Still, you could have told us that you'd been shot at and didn't know who'd done it. Get it on record," Dad said.

I couldn't tell if he was buying the story or not. I wasn't even sure what I thought of it. It seemed a bit too easy to verify. I had some pretty strong opinions about Mr. Klein, but I didn't think he was stupid.

"I had good reasons for not wanting the shooting to be investigated. One, Mr. Wilkins, my boss, doesn't like drama. Second..." He hesitated. "The woman's husband is a pretty important guy that I've worked with a lot. I really can't afford to piss him off."

"You probably should have thought about that before you had sex with his wife."

"I got a little problem when it comes to women," Klein said, sounding sincere and even a bit remorseful.

"We need her name," Dad said.

"No."

"This isn't negotiable."

"I can't give you her name. That's only going to make everyone's lives worse. Besides, I didn't *see* who shot at me. I'm only guessing that it was her. It could have been her husband, though I haven't seen any signs that he knows about us." Klein had a point. The evidence that a crime had been committed against him was all circumstantial.

Dad didn't want to let it go. I could see him going over his choices in his head. Finally, he said, "Give us the name and I give you my word that we won't contact her unless we have to."

Now it was time for Klein to consider *his* options. "Look, I'll give you her first name. If you can come back with a compelling reason, I'll give you her last name."

The look on Dad's face made it clear how irritated he was to be put into this position. But being outside of his jurisdiction and with admittedly flimsy evidence, he didn't have much leverage.

"Okay. But expect to see us again." Of course, a first name combined with some of the other clues Klein had given us would probably enable us to find out who the woman was, so Dad wasn't trading much away.

"Her name's Judith."

We asked him to recount the details of the break-up, then asked him about the shooting again. This time his description of the incident matched up with what we'd seen in the garage.

"One more question. What type of car does Judith drive?" Dad asked.

It was clear that Klein didn't want to tell him, but he couldn't seem to figure out how to avoid it without more stonewalling. "A black Mercedes."

He didn't specify the model or year and Dad didn't press him. Just getting the make and color would help when viewing camera footage.

CHAPTER FIFTEEN

My phone rang as we were getting in the truck. A glance at the caller ID told me it was Pete.

"How are the waves, dude?" he asked in the worst surfer accent I'd ever heard.

"They're rolling in," I told him.

"Are you guys, like, moving down there? 'Cause, you know, we have crime right here in Adams County that you could be working on."

"I'm sure you guys can take care of anything that comes up."

"We don't need you, but the place does feel rudderless without your dad at the helm."

"Gee, thanks. I'll tell him you miss him."

"If there's anything I can do to get him back here sooner, let me know."

"Since you asked…" I gave him Sally's number and asked him to call her and see if he could help with the backgrounds on Klein and the Leonards.

"Sure, no problem. Did I mention that there was a battle between drug dealers this weekend that resulted in one of them driving their Escalade through the rival group's front door? Darlene and I have managed to round up most of

129

them with the help of patrol. Thanks for asking. I can't hardly see over the paperwork, but I'll jump on these background checks."

I smiled at Pete's complaints. Giving each other a hard time kept us from going insane.

"Oh, yeah, Darlene's here and says she hopes a bully kicks sand in your face."

"I'm not lounging around on the beach, guys."

"Sure you aren't. I'll give this Sally person a call and see if I can help her out."

"Thanks. Save some work for me."

"Oh, trust me, pal. We're dumping every crap report we get right into your inbox," Pete said cheerily.

"You two are true friends."

After I hung up, Dad said, "Parks told me about the little drug war this weekend. By the luck of the dumb and the drunk, no one was killed. Five in the hospital." Sam Parks was the department's senior administrator and acting sheriff when Dad was out of town.

"Wouldn't mind grabbing something to drink," Dad said, pulling into the parking lot of the little store and marina. I glanced at him, suspecting that he had an ulterior motive for stopping.

Inside, Patty was behind the counter again. Dad looked around at the snacks and fishing supplies before selecting a tea from the drinks cooler. He bought a little more time looking at a rack of touristy knick-knacks, allowing the other customer in the store to finish up with his purchase of lottery tickets and beer. Finally, he approached the counter.

"How's it going?" Dad asked Patty, who gave him a big smile.

"It's Monday morning, but we're managing. How 'bout you all?"

"Same. We're still looking into that body and Mrs. Schultz's apparent suicide."

At the mention of Pauline Schultz, Patty's smile faded. "I don't understand that," she said, obvious emotion attached to her words.

"She seemed like a good person," Dad sympathized.

"Our birthdays are the same week. She was a couple years older than me, but we were both Geminis. Born just two days apart."

"You all were friends?" Dad's voice was soft and comforting.

Patty considered the question for a few moments. "Yes. Yes, we were. I mean, we didn't go places together or anything like that, but I'd like to think we were friends. A lot of times she'd come in and we'd just talk. If I had the time and Howard could watch the store, we'd go out back and sit on the dock and have a drink." Her eyes looked off into the distance, no doubt remembering some of those conversations.

"Must be hard losing a friend like that. Suicides never make any sense to the ones left behind."

Patty's eyes narrowed and she leaned forward. "I'll tell you this. If Pauline killed herself then she had a good reason. She wasn't just depressed or didn't have a reason to go on living. No, if she hung herself, it was for a rock-solid purpose."

"You have any idea what that reason might have been?"

"No, I don't," Patty said with a sigh.

"Was there anything, and I mean anything, different about her in the past week or so?"

"Maybe she seemed a bit... distracted."

"Distracted how?"

"I don't know. Maybe she looked around a bit more when she was in the store. Like she expected someone else might walk in on her at any moment."

"Would you say she was acting paranoid?"

"No, no nothing like that. Just like she was keeping an eye out, but I don't know if she expected a friend or an enemy. In some ways she seemed more... upbeat. Almost like someone who'd gotten rid of a weight that they'd been carrying around."

"Could it be that she was expecting the weight to be lifted in the future?"

"Yeah, that's possible."

Dad took out his phone and showed her the picture of Fowler. "I know you've already said that you didn't recognize the face of the dead guy, but now I've got a better photo. His name was Claude Fowler and he did heating and air work."

Patty still shook her head.

"What do you think of Blake Klein?" Dad asked suddenly and she looked up sharply.

"Why?" was her very telling response.

"Just asking."

"Don't try to fool an old fool. You've got a reason for asking."

"Yep," Dad said with a smile.

"Well, what is it?" Patty said, her lips turning up a little.

"Why don't you want to talk about him?"

"Why do you think I don't want to talk about him?"

"Because you're being as evasive as a fox with a hundred dogs chasing after him."

Now she laughed a little. "Okay, I'll show you mine first. Klein's not a man you want to get on the wrong side of."

"There's been trouble?"

"Ain't no secret. Several people have had property disputes with Klein."

"I thought it was Wilkins that owned the property."

"Most of it. But Klein has bought and sold a few places himself. And, honestly, it doesn't matter if he's protecting his property or Wilkins's. He can be pretty mean either way."

"You ever have a run-in with him?"

Patty stayed silent.

"You don't want to talk about it."

"Can't talk about it."

"Why's that?" Dad asked, puzzled.

"Part of the settlement."

"Ahhhh, I see." Dad smiled. "I promise I won't ask you

anything about that. I get that he's not your favorite person on the island. What we're looking for is a little general gossip. I'd actually prefer if you'd put your personal feelings aside. Okay?"

"Sure," Patty said.

"Have you heard any rumors about Klein being a womanizer?"

"No, not really. But then again, he runs in his own circles. It's not like I see him down at the VFW."

"Understood. How many people do you think might be angry enough to take a few potshots at him?"

"Including us or not?"

"Let's say not."

"Joking aside, I can think of a dozen people that were mad enough at one time or another who'd have been thrilled to make him crap in his pants. Maybe only one or two might try and hit their target."

"Care to name names?"

"Nope. You'll have to arrest me for obstruction or harboring a criminal or whatever it is you all do."

Dad and Patty both were having a grand old time with the chitchat, but I wasn't sure if Dad was getting anything out of it.

A young couple, clearly tourists with their bathing suits and sunglasses, came into the store. Dad decided to wrap things up. "I'll take a rain check on arresting you. Is your husband out back?"

"Better be," she said, watching the new customers pick through the suntan lotions.

"Mind if we step out back and have a word with him?"

"He's probably washing down the boats."

We found Howard doing exactly that. "What's the law doing here?" he said after we'd gotten his attention.

"Just wanted to talk to you for a minute, if you don't mind?" Dad was in his laid-back, friend-to-all mode. It was clear that he liked Patty and Howard.

"Sure thing. I could use a break. These rental boats are a

pain in the ass. I'd get rid of them if they didn't make us so much money. Of course, we'd make a lot more if we didn't have to pay so darn much for insurance," he grumbled good-naturedly as he rolled up the hose.

"I bet you get some kooks," Dad agreed.

"Don't even get me started. We've been lucky so far, but I told Patty that one of these days a boat's not going to come back and they'll find it out there half submerged or upside down. I try and cull out the dumbest ones. I turn away about half the folks. They're drunk or stupid or the weather's too bad. Now, don't get me wrong. I got some regulars that I'm always glad to see. I know they'll bring the boat back on time, in one piece and reasonably clean. But I bet you didn't come here to talk about my boat business."

"Sorry to say, but no."

"Come on. Let's sit over here out of the sun."

We took seats around a picnic table with an umbrella sticking out of the middle.

"What's on your mind?" Howard asked, sitting back and stretching his feet out. Few people can be that relaxed when talking to law enforcement.

"We've got two dead bodies and we're trying to help Chief Sullivan figure out what happened to those folks," Dad explained.

Howard made a face. "Horrible about Pauline. She was one nice lady. I know she had a lot of money, but you'd never know it meeting her. She was just as down-home as you could want. Patty's taking it real hard."

"One of the big questions we have to answer is, did she really commit suicide? What do you think?"

Howard took his time. "I just don't know. I want to say there's no way she'd ever do that, but…" He hesitated.

"What?"

"I don't know. It's nothing I can put my finger on. She just seemed melancholy. No, that's not the right word. Worried, maybe. I'm not going to be much help. It's taken me almost ten years to learn Patty's moods. Still get them wrong sometimes."

"I've also got a better photo of the other victim." Dad showed him the DMV photo of Fowler and told Howard his name.

"Nope, doesn't ring any bells."

"We talked to Patty and she said there'd been some trouble between you all and Mr. Klein."

At the mention of the man's name, Howard sat up. I swear every muscle in his face clenched.

"We don't want to get you into trouble over the court settlement…"

"Hell with that. The man's a…" Howard stuttered, trying to find the right word to describe Klein. "I can't think of a word bad enough. He claimed that… Hell, come on, I'll show you."

He got up and we followed him to a wooden fence that was meant to keep people from bypassing the shop when they were going to the marina.

"Here's where our property line is," Howard said, tapping the fence. "Or at least where we *thought* the property line was. Our deed and our survey specified that this was the property line. But, years ago, someone had screwed up a survey on the property next door. We're talking about sixty years ago, right after World War II. Anyway, Klein bought the property next door and he got a deed that said the property line was actually twelve feet inside this fence. You can see that would put it right up against our store. He said he didn't realize the error when he bought the property and showed us all these plans he'd had drawn up based on the faulty survey lines. We said we'd work with him, but the next morning that son of a bitch had a crew out here putting up a chain link fence along the disputed property line. Look, you can see where they dug right through our asphalt to put in the posts."

Howard stopped talking and leaned against the wall. He was breathing so heavily I thought he might pass out on us.

"Would you like me to go get you some water or

something?" I asked.

"No, I'll be fine. I just... It just makes me so angry. We talked to our lawyer and were told that Klein would have an argument, which seemed crazy to me since everyone admitted that Klein's survey had been done in error. But the lawyer said that since the error had been with the laying of the meridian or something like that, then Klein could claim to be a victim.

"Anyway, once we realized we could be in trouble, we made Klein a reasonable offer. Bam! He refused it without a thought and asked for more. We wasted a good bit of money on lawyers before we just gave Klein most of what he wanted. Almost killed me. I wanted to fight him to the death, but Patty's wiser than me. She told me that the hospital bills alone wouldn't be worth it. She was right. Fighting him would have killed me. Once it was all said and done, he acted like we were all neighbors again. Money is all that man cares about. He's done worse to others. At least he left us with enough to make a go of it. Sullivan told me he thought Klein didn't want to wipe out the only store on the island, so he just milked us for what he could."

"What's your opinion of Wilkins?" I asked.

"I don't have one. I've seen him dozens of times at functions, and he's come by and filled his boat up, but that's it. Friendly enough. Nothing more. Just friendly enough. But I know Klein's in his employ, so I got to think there's something wrong with the man. Anybody that would keep a guy like Klein around has to approve of the things he does."

I nodded, thinking the same thing. "Do you know the Leonards?" I asked.

"Sure. Bob and... Never can remember his wife's name. Starts with a G or something."

"Courtney."

"Yeah, that's it. Courtney spelled with a G," Howard said with a grin.

"How well do you know them?"

"Not well enough to get her first name without help.

They're regulars in the store. Always buy their lottery tickets on Friday afternoon. Bob fills up his boat. We've never broken bread with them, if that's what you mean."

"Did they know Mrs. Schultz?" I asked.

Howard pursed his lips. "I don't think so. I mean, I'm sure that they would know her to see her, but I doubt it went any further than that."

"One last question. Can you think of anyone that knows Klein pretty well who might be willing to give us some dirt on him?" Dad asked.

"That's easy. Luke Garner. He puts out a little advertising sheet, calls it *The Pelican Brief*. Told him he'd better be careful or John Grisham will sue his ass. Anyway, he puts in some gossip and local news articles every month. Thinks he's like the guys who busted Nixon. You can pick up a copy in the store."

We thanked him and waved to Patty as we walked past, stopping just long enough at the door to pick up a copy of *The Pelican Brief.*

CHAPTER SIXTEEN

I found the address of the paper on the inside first page. Garner's house was one of the older ones on the island. Standing on eight-foot posts and made of cypress turned grey with age, it was festooned with old fishing nets and harkened back to simpler times on the coast.

As a law enforcement officer, I've seldom been welcomed as warmly on a cold call as we were by Luke Garner. He was in his early fifties with a Hemingway beard. With his T-shirt, cargo shorts and flip-flops, he would have looked right at home on stage at a Jimmy Buffett concert.

"Excellent! Chief Sullivan never keeps me in the loop. I keep telling him we should work together. Man, this is great. I've been trying to get a line on all the action going on this past weekend. A body washing up and then poor Pauline Schultz hanging herself. How sad is that? It's crazy, man. But now you're here to give me all the 411. Can't beat that."

The interior of the house was one big open room combining the kitchen, living room and bedroom. There were two doors down on one end, one of which I assumed led to a bathroom. The décor took the word eclectic to a new dimension. The walls were covered floor to ceiling with old photographs, some of them framed and a lot of them not. There were also newspaper articles and other memorabilia mixed in with the photos.

Dad and I were both drawn to the items on the walls. Most of the photos looked like they'd been taken between the late 1930s on up through the '70s. The early ones were of soldiers, airmen, nurses, WACs, WAVES and representatives of almost every other military service from World War II.

"Those are my grandfather's pictures. He was a photographer for the Army during the war. Later he went to work for the *Pensacola Tribune.*"

"These were all taken around here?" Dad asked.

"Oh, yeah. He was stationed here. This part of Florida was a major training hub during the war. Grandpa documented most of it. Have you been to the Camp Gordon Johnson Museum? I gave them some of his stuff for their collection. It's great that they're preserving the history."

I'd wandered down to the end of the room near the doors. Recently developed photos were hanging up to dry near an open window. Garner came up behind me as I stared closely at one of the pictures.

"Isn't he something? I saw that beast down at the dog beach on the mainland yesterday. She ain't too shabby either."

It was a photo of Mauser standing knee-deep in the Gulf water with Cara next to him, holding onto his leash and wearing an expression of pure joy. I thought about explaining, but instead just smiled and nodded. I had to agree with his assessment of Cara.

"We wanted to pick your brain a little," Dad said.

"Pick away, man. As long as I can get a few of my questions answered," he said amiably. "Sit down and make yourselves comfortable." He pulled a pen from behind his ear and sat down on the couch. "Let me get your names again and stuff." He picked up a pad from a pile of books and papers on the coffee table.

Dad and I looked at each other, then took chairs across from him. The guy was certainly a character. We gave him a full explanation of who we were and how we'd come to be involved in the local cases.

"Father and son. Cool. My dad was kind of a wet blanket, wanted me to be a lawyer. That wasn't for me. I was lucky, though. Grampa was behind me every step of the way. Life's too short, was his motto. Said he took photos of ten thousand guys who never came back from the war. Said he'd made up his mind right then never to waste a day doing something he hated."

"Your grandfather still alive?" Dad asked.

"No, he died five years ago. Right here." He indicated the couch while I kind of hoped he just meant the room in general. "I came and stayed with him for his last couple of years. We started *The Pelican Brief* together."

"What can you tell us about Blake Klein?"

"Wow, I wish I could print some of the stuff I've heard. That dude is mean as a snake. He's cheated a lot of folks." He squinted and looked up at the ceiling fan. "Well, cheated might be too harsh a word. Let's say he's found ways to squeeze money out of everybody he can. He threatened me once. Made me print a retraction. Told me if I ever printed anything libelous about him again, he'd close me down and kick me off the island."

"You think he meant it?"

"Oh, yeah. I don't even put his name in the paper anymore."

"Do you know of anyone who would want to kill him?"

"Too many to name. Like I said, he's done some damage to folks. Wait! The shooting!" He slapped himself in the forehead. "I heard someone shot at Wilkins, but it was really Klein, right? Well, that makes sense. Duh!"

"What about women? Have you heard any rumors about him and women?"

"A few. Mostly people disgusted that someone would go out with the guy. But he's shown up at some of the community stuff, like the Fourth of July fireworks, with a woman from time to time. Usually pretty and young. I always figured he paid for them."

"Would you know any of the people he worked with?" I asked.

"Absolutely. Before he slammed a cease-and-desist order on me, I'd built up a pretty big file on him." Luke got up and went over to a wall lined with old grey filing cabinets. "Gramps loved paper files. When you just want to flip through your research or lay it all out, there really isn't anything better," he said, pulling out a couple of file folders that were each over four inches thick.

He took them over to a large table that could have seated ten people and shoved the piles of papers that were on it down to the end so that about half the table was exposed. He opened the folders and started laying out papers. "I have a file on Wilkins and one on Klein. From what I can tell, Wilkins uses Klein to keep his hands clean. I can't tell how much of Klein's actions Wilkins knows about."

"We're looking for a man Klein does business with who'd have a wife with the first name of Judith," Dad said, scanning the papers in front of us.

"Judy, Judith. Rings a bell. You say Klein works with this guy?"

"He said that the guy was important to his business. Something like that."

"Ohhhhh," Luke said, a smile spreading across his face. "I bet I know who we're talking about." He dug through the photos, news clippings and printed articles, then pulled out a report about a county commission meeting. "I bet he's talking about that guy."

He pointed to a photo of a man sitting behind an officious-looking desk. The name plate in front of him read: *Brad Murray—Commissioner.* "His wife is Judith Murray. Quite the looker. Mostly arm candy, from what I can tell. Murray brings her out for special occasions."

Dad and I looked at each other. This was getting deep if it involved a county commissioner.

We spent the next hour telling Luke what we could about

Fowler's murder and the death of Pauline Schultz. In turn, he gave us lots of island gossip. Evidently he had an endless supply and, finally, we just had to stand up and tell him we needed to go.

"This is all pretty mind-blowing," Luke said as he walked us to the door.

My watch and my stomach told me it was time for lunch. We headed back to the house, where Genie was making sandwiches. I took mine to the table to check out their progress on the word puzzle. I tried not to drop parts of my sandwich on the glued-together pieces, which wasn't easy since Mauser kept nudging at my arm.

"Go away, chow hound," I said, turning to him with my best angry grimace that he completely ignored. "You're a famous model now. You need to watch your weight," I told him.

"What?" Cara asked with a puzzled expression on her face.

"You too," I said and then explained about the photographs.

"Oh, him. Nice guy. He'd fit right in at the co-op with my parents," she joked.

I turned back to the paper strips. Suddenly a group of words on different pieces of paper jumped out at me. *Pharmacy, drug, warnings, side effects.*

"Eureka!" I said, while mentally kicking myself for not making the connection earlier.

Mauser took advantage of my excitement to jump up and grab the rest of my sandwich off of my plate. I chased him to the couch, where he buried his face full of sandwich into the cushions to keep me from getting it back. I struggled with him for a minute and managed to pry a bit of it out of his jaws. I was pretty sure that the salami wouldn't do a thing for the dog's already legendary flatulence.

"What was your eureka moment?" Cara asked after I'd thrown the remnants of my sandwich into the trash and made myself another.

"I know what all of this has to do with," I said, indicating the shredded papers. "Well, most of it."

"What? Spit it out. If this was a mystery movie of the week, someone would shoot you through the window right now and we'd never learn what you discovered," Dad said.

"Medicine. Her two husbands' illnesses. Maybe the accusations that she killed them, or at least assisted them in taking their own lives."

Dad looked down and started picking through the papers. "You could be right. But that—" He was interrupted by his phone. "Sullivan," Dad told us, looking at the number.

He answered and listened to Sullivan for a moment. I could hear his voice, but couldn't make out anything other than the obvious fact that the man was very excited.

"Calm down," Dad told him. "Seal off the property and call for backup. We're on our way." Dad hung up, his face positively ashen. "They've found a husband and wife murdered in their own house."

As Dad and I made our way to a modern three-story beach house facing the Gulf, we passed an unusual amount of traffic on the island's two-lane road.

"Damn it, look," Dad said, pointing to an SUV heading in the other direction. It had a pile of beach gear and suitcases precariously strapped to the roof.

"I guess word has gotten out."

"People are leaving." Dad got on his phone and called Sullivan. "You need to set up a roadblock and at least get the names and addresses of everyone scurrying off of the island. Okay, well, that's something. Yep, I can see you now." He hung up and turned to me. "A state trooper is stationed at the bridge."

Sullivan was standing next to his old patrol car, looking very much alone as he watched guests and residents alike drive past, cars stuffed with kids and luggage.

We parked one house away. Sullivan had properly strung crime scene tape across the front yard so that thoughtless first responders wouldn't obscure any evidence by parking in the driveway or on the lawn.

"It's bad," Sullivan said, a look of disbelief on his face. "Duncan's people are on their way."

"Who found the bodies?" I asked.

"The neighbors. Ed and Jessica Holden. They were surprised when the Fernandezes weren't home last night. They tried calling them all morning but couldn't get an answer, so they got worried and came over to check."

Dad and I both wanted to view the crime scene, especially with the chance that Duncan might try to keep us out later, but we couldn't in good conscience go in before the crime scene techs arrived. We forced ourselves to wait and I took advantage of the moment, pulling Dad aside.

"You can't piss Duncan off," I told him and the look on his face made it clear that the warning was necessary. When his only response was to stare at me, I went on, "Seriously, I know how angry you are at him. He's a jerk and an idiot. But if you want to have a chance at solving these murders and getting Jerome out of jail, you've got to get a handle on your anger."

I felt silly treating him like a child, but I knew that it had been a long time since he'd had to kowtow to someone else. He ground his teeth and stared at me. While I knew that his frustration and anger weren't directed at me, I still found it very intimidating.

"I can't see him," Dad finally said, his tone cold and hard. "If I see him strutting around pretending to be a law enforcement officer after he's coerced a confession out of a vulnerable young man, I don't know what I'll say."

"Then you need to leave." In the distance we could hear the sound of approaching sirens. I was sure that Duncan wouldn't be far behind them.

"You're right." Dad walked back to Sullivan. "Do I have your permission to go interview the neighbors who found the bodies?" Seeing Dad in a position where he couldn't exert personal authority was a bit unnerving.

"Sure, yeah," Sullivan answered, still in the daze caused by seeing his world radically change in only a couple of days.

"Which house?"

Sullivan pointed to a house two doors down on the left and Dad marched off. I decided to stay.

Within ten minutes there were two patrol cars, Duncan's SUV and a crime scene van parked in front of the house. I hung in the background, watching the techs go inside to start taking photos and filming the scene. Duncan didn't even acknowledge Sullivan for the first ten minutes. When he did come over, he was full of attitude.

"I just want to be clear. I'm in charge of this investigation. Beginning to end. Understood?" Duncan was standing well inside of Sullivan's personal space.

"Yes, of course," Sullivan said. The most recent murders had destroyed his will to resist.

"I don't want you or any of your... friends meddling." He glanced over at me. "Understood?" he said, still looking at me.

I refused to engage him, pretending that I wasn't listening.

"I understand," Sullivan said, his voice lifeless.

We've got our work cut out for us, I thought.

Apparently unable to think of any other asshole comments to make, Duncan finally wandered off, talking on his radio.

I came over and stood almost as close to Sullivan as Duncan had.

"You need to snap out of this. I know that what's happened is horrible, but if you leave it to that idiot to find the murderer then you're not fulfilling your responsibility to this community. A community that you swore to protect and serve." I saw a flicker of life behind his eyes. "And without your help, we can't do much."

"But..." he started, then lost his train of thought again.

"Come on," I encouraged him. "You've got to rally. If not for yourself, then for Jerome. The man is in jail, possibly in mortal jeopardy, until someone takes on that idiot Duncan."

"I'm way out of my depth."

"Yeah, you probably are. So you know what you need to do? Swim. When you're in over your head, you better damn well start swimming."

Sullivan looked at me with eyes that were a bit more focused. "I don't know what I can do."

"You said that you know one of the crime scene techs that doesn't like Duncan. Someone who might do you a favor."

"Yeah."

"Is he here?"

Sullivan turned to look at the techs in their protective outfits. "That's him, Quinn." He pointed toward an older man with a sizeable potbelly. I took out my phone, turned it to vibrate so there'd be no chance of anyone hearing it ring, and handed it to Sullivan.

"I want you to discreetly go over and ask him to use my phone to film the crime scene." I looked around and saw Duncan walking into the house. "Now's a good time. Go on." I gave Sullivan a little push.

For a moment I wasn't sure if he'd go through with it, then I saw him walk up to take Quinn aside. I saw my phone change hands, followed by a nodding of heads. Then Quinn picked up a case of equipment and walked back inside the house.

Forty-five minutes later, while Duncan was preoccupied with the pair of news vans that had shown up, Sullivan sidled up to Quinn and got my phone back.

"Thanks," I said as he handed it back to me.

"Don't thank me, thank Quinn." He glanced over at Duncan, who'd finished with the reporters. "But maybe not right now."

"I better go get Dad before Duncan sends someone over

to interview the Holdens. We'll call you."

Sullivan nodded, looking like he was going to fall back into his introspective lethargy.

I sighed. "Look, you have to pick yourself up and move forward. We need you to stay as close to this investigation as possible. You're going to be our main source of information. You don't really want to turn this all over to Duncan, do you?"

I was more used to being on the receiving end of the Vince Lombardi pep talks than giving them, but I must have done okay. Sullivan straightened his shoulders and nodded.

Dad was coming out of the Holdens' house just as I reached their lawn. I waved him down the street away from the crime scene.

"Duncan is all over it," I told him.

Dad's jaw was set as he looked down the street toward the spot where Duncan's Escalade was parked. Luckily there were enough other cars parked along the street that we could screen ourselves and avoid a possible run-in with Duncan.

"Keep your eyes on the prize. A blowout with Duncan, especially with the news crews here, would just result in us getting kicked out of the county or arrested for obstruction."

Dad gave me a cold look. "This role reversal where you're the voice of reason is annoying as hell."

"Let's hope the world gets back to normal soon. Here, this might cheer you up." I took out my phone. "I've got footage of the crime scene."

"Maybe you *are* my son." Dad actually smiled.

We slunk behind the parked vehicles and made it down to Dad's truck. The three-point turn to get out was a little tricky, and I kept waiting for Duncan to come running over or send one of his deputies to stop us, but we managed to make a clean getaway.

CHAPTER SEVENTEEN

Back at the house we had just managed to figure out how to transfer the video to my laptop when Dad's phone rang. It was Jay Moreno. Dad put him on speakerphone.

"Good news and bad news," Jay reported.

"Good news first," Dad said.

"Jerome's public defender was able to get me in to meet with him before the hearing and Jerome agreed to let me represent him. So I was able to be with him at the hearing."

"Bad news?"

"It didn't do him much good. He's being held on the charge of second-degree murder and grand theft. His bail was set at half a million dollars. Needless to say, that's not going to happen."

"Grand theft?"

"It appears that Jerome had several things belonging to Fowler, including a laptop, in his possession when he was arrested."

"I'm sure Fowler gave or loaned them to him."

"You're preaching to the choir. Unfortunately that's the motive they're going with. And with both Fowler and Jerome being loners, it's going to be hard to come up with evidence that Fowler willingly gave the items to Jerome."

I heard an odd sound. Dad was growling under his breath. Mauser must have heard it too. He crawled off of the couch, put his big snout up in the air and let loose with several loud barks.

"What's up, Mauser!" Jay shouted from the phone, causing Mauser to really have a meltdown, barking back at the phone. Jay laughed hysterically. He wasn't a dog guy, but he got a kick out of Mauser and people's reactions to him.

Cara came over and managed to calm Mauser down with a back rub and a few treats.

Jay turned serious again. "There isn't much I can do at this point except try and instill some hope in Jerome and Mrs. Peters. By the way, she's a great person and is going to be a huge asset to Jerome as a character witness and to keep his spirits up. That's important. I've seen prison cause some folks with limited resources to pretty much curl up inside themselves and disappear. That makes it very hard to mount a strong defense."

"Let's hope it doesn't come to a trial," Dad said.

"Hope for the best, plan for the worst. If you don't have anything else for me, I've got to go meet another client," Jay said and we signed off.

Cara and Genie joined us at the laptop. "Can we watch?" Cara asked.

"I don't think you really want to," I said.

"Are you sure?" Dad looked at Genie with his eyebrows raised.

"The more eyes the better, right?" Cara said. "You aren't going to have too many other people to discuss it with."

I hadn't really thought about that, but she had a point. It wasn't like I could call up the crime scene techs and ask them questions. It would just be Sullivan, Sally, Dad and me unless we showed the footage to someone else.

Dad could tell that I was getting ready to give in to the request. He turned and faced them. "Let's be clear here. What we're doing is a felony. This is a pretty cut-and-dried case of obstruction of justice. By illegally filming the crime scene, there is the possibility that we could let information leak that would make it harder for law enforcement to investigate and prosecute this case." He delivered this speech like he was addressing a class of cadets.

"Isn't knowledge of the film enough to get us charged? Assuming we don't inform Duncan immediately," Cara said with just an ounce of snark.

"I'm not sure I like you," Dad said, though his tone implied just the opposite. "Fine, suit yourselves." He gave Genie a small smile. "But it won't be pretty. Remember, this will be something you can't unsee."

After nods all around, I hit play.

The video started outside the house. It was taken at a rather odd angle and it took me a second to figure out that it was due to the fact that Quinn was holding the phone cupped in his hand. Luckily, the guy had meat hooks for hands. Only occasionally would a finger or thumb get in the way.

He walked up the stairs to the second and main floor of the house. The elaborate front door was propped open with a crime scene bag. The house must have cost a small fortune. Everything from floor to ceiling looked high end. Nothing had been disturbed until Quinn entered what was either a library or an office. The room was paneled in dark wood, making the lighting on the footage problematic. But the open safe behind the desk stood out clearly. Sitting at the desk, slumped a bit against the wall, was the body of a man with part of his head missing.

"Quinn, give us a hand," a tech off screen said. What came next were disorienting images and then darkness. *"Yeah, hold that. No, little to the right."*

"We're in his pocket," I said, though I'm sure everyone else had figured this out.

After a few more minutes of blackness, we got a good view of the inside of the safe. Judging by the powder covering everything, it had already been dusted for prints. There wasn't much inside, just a few empty jewelry cases.

The rest of the house was immaculate. Everything seemed normal, if a bit obsessively clean, until we got to the master bedroom.

"Oh!" Genie said, putting her hand to her mouth.

"That's sick," Cara breathed and I took her hand.

The body of a woman was lying on the bed. Her legs were spread and her clothes were in disarray. A huge blossom of red around the woman's head marred the bright white bed linens. To the side of the bed, a few of the drawers had been dumped from a dresser, including one that held some jewelry. It was impossible to tell if anything was missing.

Quinn stepped into an elevator. We heard someone on a radio call him and he answered that he'd be right out. He exited the elevator into the garage. Everything there was neat as well. I had the irreverent thought that folks who lived like this must have maids to clean their garages. This one even had indoor/outdoor carpet. Two cars were neatly parked—a BMW and a Jaguar convertible.

As Quinn approached the cottage-style back door that led out into the yard facing the beach, it was possible to see a neat circle cut out of the window. Outside the door, inside a pot of geraniums, was the round piece of glass that had been removed from the window pane. Quinn recorded the walk leading up to the door and down to the beach and then the video ended.

"Murder, rape and robbery," I said, looking at Dad quizzically.

"Staged rape. Possible robbery. Definitely murder," he said.

"Staged?" Genie asked, and I could tell that it bothered her to even think about the bedroom scene.

"I wish you hadn't seen that." Dad squeezed her hand.

"It's okay," she said grimly. "Why do you say it was staged?"

"Too neat. The bed wasn't messed up at all. Also, it's odd that he shot her like that. I would expect strangulation or stabbing or, if she had been shot, that it would have occurred somewhere else."

"You don't know that she wasn't strangled," I pointed out.

"True." Dad said. "The gunshot coming as the *coup de grâce*. Possibly."

"I still don't quite understand why you think the scene was staged," Genie said.

"Me either," Cara chimed in.

Dad explained, "What it's meant to look like is that the woman was pushed back on the bed and raped while the man held a gun in his hand, and that he shot her immediately afterward."

"Okay, so…?"

"Most rapists don't want to hold a gun in their hand during the act. First of all, they usually use knives or their hands to control their victims because it's more personal and instills more fear. Fear and power are often the main things a rapist gets out of it. They also don't like using a gun that close to a victim because it would be pretty easy for the victim to get ahold of it and turn it on their attacker."

"Maybe."

"Think of it this way. If you took a knife away from a potential rapist, he'd have a much better chance of taking it back from you or simply escaping than if you were able to turn a gun on him," Dad said.

"I can see that. Maybe he put the gun down, attacked her and then shot her," Cara suggested.

"Possibly. But there would be some time between him finishing the attack and retrieving the gun to shoot her."

"Right."

"So she would have probably moved," I said. "Curled up on the bed, or tried to roll away or stand up. But this makes it look like she just laid there. Look at the fact that the bed isn't messed up at all except for the blood stain. I think what really happened is that she was pushed back on the bed, shot and then her clothes were half pulled off."

"If he's someone who was trying to stage the scene and really thought about it first, he might have hit her inner thighs and penetrated her with something to add physical signs of a sexual assault to the body." Dad saw the sickened expressions on Cara's and Genie's faces. "I'm sorry. We just have to take a clinical look at the evidence."

"I know," Genie said, her eyes on the floor.

"Did you all see anything unusual on the video?" I asked, trying to get them to think about something other than the sexual assault.

"I don't know." Cara looked thoughtful. "The house was so neat. And the hole cut in the back door looked like someone from a James Bond movie had done it."

"Good eye," Dad praised her. "The break-in was very professional."

"So, if he was a professional burglar then why would he break in when people were home?" Genie asked

"When I interviewed the Holdens, they claimed that the Fernandezes were supposed to be out of town until Sunday afternoon."

"When did the murders occur?" Genie asked.

"Probably before last night. Mr. Holden said he'd looked over several times during the evening to see if the lights had come on. He wanted to ask Mr. Fernandez a question about some stocks he wanted to buy, but he didn't want to disturb him while they were on a trip. Holden had planned on coming over as soon as he saw that they were home. Holden really wanted to get the stock trade done before the market opened this morning. He said that Fernandez was a real wizard when it came to the market."

While Dad talked, I texted Sullivan, asking if he'd heard an estimated time of death for the Fernandezes. "They probably died between forty-eight and twenty-four hours ago," I read the texted response.

"Hey, I thought of something else that's odd," Cara said.

"What's that?" Dad asked her.

"They were dressed in casual clothes. People like that

would have dressed up if they were going to go out. But he had on a polo shirt and slacks while she was wearing a blouse and shorts."

"So?"

Cara's brows knit together as she tried to think it through. "The house was so clean."

"Maybe they were just very neat people," Dad said.

"That could be, but they were dressed like they were hanging out at the house. And nothing was out of place. I mean, nothing. There wasn't a glass on the coffee table or a dish in the sink. There wasn't a book or magazine on the couch. Nothing in the office looked like it was being read or used. *Nothing* was out of place."

"Come to think of it, I didn't see any phones or pads lying around. No electronic devices at all," I said.

"Why would a high-end burglar steal their phones and computers?" Cara asked.

"They wouldn't," Dad said simply.

"This was definitely staged," I said.

My phone buzzed with another text from Sullivan. He had shared a link with a headline that read: *Sheriff Discusses Recent Murders.*

"Incoming," I told them, forwarding the link to my laptop so we could all see it.

The video segment was from a Panama City station, but there were multiple microphones being held out to Sheriff Duncan as he talked.

"At this time we are confident that the murderer of Claude Fowler is in custody. These murders," he indicated the Fernandez house behind him, "are unrelated. What we know about the Fernandez murders at this time is that they appear to be a case of an interrupted burglary. The intruder subsequently killed Dana and Ralph Fernandez. We have the following description of a suspect: he is of average height and weight, wearing a black hoodie and jeans. A forensic artist is working with the witness now and we'll get that composite sketch out to you as soon as it is completed.

"Meanwhile, we're going to be reviewing all of the burglaries that have occurred in the area over the last six months, as well as anyone who has a record for similar offenses who's living in the area. I'll say one more thing. It is regrettable that the island chose to create an amateurish security force when they were having problems several years ago. If they had left it in the hands of the sheriff's office, these murders probably could have been avoided."

"Bastard threw Jerome, Sullivan *and* Sally under the bus," Genie said in disgust. Dad stood up and pulled her close to his side.

"We have our work cut out for us. Actually, it might be easier now with Duncan off on a wild goose chase," Dad said.

His bravado was impressive. I wasn't feeling quite so sanguine with our time on the island passing away like sand through an hourglass and with no official standing in the investigation. As though to punctuate this last thought, Dad's phone started to buzz angrily.

"It's Duncan," he, said looking at the caller ID. "Howdy," he said cheerily.

"Don't you howdy me, you intruding son of a bitch! I just found out that you interviewed the Holdens." Dad was holding the phone away from his ear and Duncan was yelling so loudly that it sounded like he was on speakerphone. "If I find out that you even look at another witness in this case, I'll put you and that incompetent son of yours in jail. And I mean in jail, not some holding cell. You hear me?"

"Loud and clear, boss," Dad said insolently.

"I've recorded this phone call. You hear me?" Duncan repeated.

"Yes, I can practically hear you without the phone," Dad said, and I could almost feel the heat rising on the other end.

"Keep it up and I'll send a couple of men to arrest you right now."

"For what?" Dad pushed.

"For obstruction of justice to start with. Interfering with

an investigation and any other damn thing I want. I'm the big dog in this county, asshole."

"Are you still recording? 'Cause I am," Dad lied.

Silence followed until the phone went to a dial tone.

Dad looked over at Mauser who was looking up at him with a wrinkled brow. Dad walked over to him and ruffled his ears. "Don't worry. You're the biggest dog in whatever county you're in. Don't let that mean man tell you any different."

I wasn't sure whether to be optimistic about the strange, playful mood that Dad was in or to worry that it was signaling some sort of psychotic break.

Dad looked up at all of us. "I'm going to make that man eat every single word." His tone told me all I needed to know about Dad's psyche. He was pissed off and ready to fight.

"Brave words, captain," I said. He gave me a look that said I was being a sarcastic ass. "But I'm proud to be a member of the crew," I added, extending the metaphor and letting him know that I was supportive. I certainly wanted to see Duncan face down in a cow patty.

We all agreed that we needed a break. Cara and I went upstairs and stood outside on the deck off of our bedroom. Looking out over the sawgrass and the peaceful water, it seemed hard to imagine that a murderer was loose on the island.

"I really need to head home. Dr. Barnhill doesn't have anyone else who can cover for me tomorrow," Cara said sadly.

"I know. It's okay. Dad has to be back at work on Wednesday morning and I really don't see how I can stay down here playing cowboy on my own. I'll just ride back up with him and Mauser," I said, knowing how much it would eat at Dad to have to leave things unresolved on the island. Especially if it meant leaving Jerome in jail.

"Is there any chance you all can figure this out by then?"

"I don't know." I shrugged.

"What a mess."

"Go home, take care of Ivy and Alvin. Don't worry. We'll be fine."

"That's easier said than done."

A few kisses and a long hug later, I helped her pack and we went back downstairs. It was already three o'clock. Genie and Dad had had a similar discussion and she had decided to go back with Cara since she had to be at work on Tuesday afternoon.

"And we have to leave here by six on Wednesday morning," Dad sighed as we watched the two women drive away.

"Let's try not taking it down to the wire."

CHAPTER EIGHTEEN

Sullivan showed up half an hour later.

"The highway patrol had to pull their guy off of the bridge, so Sally's up there taking names for another two hours until one of Duncan's deputies can spell her off," he told us.

We showed him the crime scene video and shared what we'd discussed. He said the place seemed even cleaner when you were in it.

"It was weird as all hell. Everything in place with not a speck of dust and then, bam, a dead body. Not an experience I want to repeat."

"Let's go over the crimes again," Dad said. He led us over to the coffee table. On sheets of paper he wrote out the names of suspects and the individual crimes. After laying them all out on the table, he began to try to put them into some sort of order.

"Let's start out with the deaths. I'm willing to consider that the shooting was just a random event that happened to occur while the other events were unfolding. So, first, we have Pauline Schultz hiring Claude Fowler for some clandestine purpose. This event leads to Fowler crossing paths with someone who decided that they had to kill him.

With Fowler dead, Pauline, either out of desperation or despair, destroys old medical records that related to both of her husbands' deaths and then hangs herself. Probably about that same time, someone murders the Fernandezes."

"What if Pauline killed the Fernandezes and then killed herself?" I suggested wildly.

"I find it hard to imagine her killing two people like that," Sullivan said. *Does that mean you* could *see her killing one person?* I wondered.

"Depending on what the coroner comes back with, I guess it's possible. Murder/suicides are not unheard of. And the scene had an old-time mystery movie feel to it. What you might expect an older woman would imagine a crime scene looks like. She could probably get the drop on them because they wouldn't expect her to be capable of it. Her son certainly thought she was a cold-blooded killer." Dad seemed to consider it. "You know, I'm not willing to discount the possibility. Let's entertain the theory."

"What about Fowler? Are you suggesting that she could have killed him too?" Sullivan asked.

"I can come up with two possibilities. One, she hired him to solve some problem for her, but, in the process of working for her, he found out something that gave him some leverage over her. Maybe he discovered clear evidence that she had killed her late husbands so she had to kill him," I speculated.

"I don't like that one," Dad said. "Being able to surprise the Fernandezes seems more plausible than doing the same with Fowler. Especially if he was trying to blackmail her. In that case, I'd imagine that he'd be pretty hyper-alert around her."

"Okay. She hired Fowler to handle the Fernandezes. But the Fernandezes kill Fowler in self-defense, so Pauline decides to take care of them personally then she exits the building herself," I offered.

Dad squinted, deep in thought. "I don't hate it. But we'd need to come up with some real evidence before I'd buy the whole cow. Such as, what motive would she have had for killing Ralph and Dana Fernandez?"

"Are we sure that Pauline was a suicide?" I asked.

Sullivan answered that one. "When I was with Dr. Thomlinson, I pushed that issue pretty hard. He said there were a few injuries that occurred at the time of her death, but that they were all consistent with her stepping off of the balcony with the noose around her neck. But they also could have been the result of someone struggling with her while they put the noose around her neck and pushed her off."

"But wouldn't she have scratched them or had injuries to her hands?"

"There was a soft spot at the back of her head that, while it wouldn't have rendered her unconscious, could have dazed a woman of her age enough to make it easy to do the rest. Again, the wound to the back of the head could just as easily been caused by her hitting her head on the railing after she stepped off the balcony."

"Great. I thought we had that more in the certain column," I said, feeling frustrated.

"I wouldn't move it from suicide to murder yet. We all saw the scene. My experience says that was a suicide," Dad said.

"Okay, what about the son who hated his mother?" I asked.

"But he was in New York," Sullivan piped up.

"It wouldn't be the first time that someone hired a killer."

"Then he got a good one," Dad said. "I know I'm the one who suggested it, but I really can't see it in this case. The best you can get out of most hired killers is a botched job where the wrong people get killed. This would have to have been an expert job to leave so little evidence."

"I know," I said thoughtfully. "But all that money is a lot of cream on that hate cake." I held up my hand, pulling out my phone to call Sally.

"Hey, how do you like working traffic?"

"You can't see it, but I'm shooting you a bird right now.

Actually, there's not much going on right this minute. The people that were going to leave have already left and no one else is coming to vacation on Murder Island. To be fair, though, it *is* Monday."

"Did you ever get the chance to do the background check on Owen Lampert?"

"I was working with that investigator, Pete, from your office. He's quite a hoot."

"That's Pete."

"I sent him what I had and he said that he had a couple more searches he could run. I sent him the stuff on the Leonards and Klein too."

"Great. We're at the house if you aren't too tired when you get off."

"I'll come by. It's that or go home to the kids and a grumpy husband."

"Hey, don't destroy your marriage for the job," I said seriously.

She laughed. "He's fine. He was just unlucky enough to have picked this week to take off from work. Serves him right. He'd planned on fishing all week."

I hung up with Sally and called Pete.

"If you keep bothering me, how am I ever going to finish the three jobs you sent to me?" was how he answered his phone.

"I doubt you're being worked to death. Did you get that information on our guys?"

"I didn't know there was a deadline," he said, only half joking.

"There is a very real deadline," I said. I went on and explained how things were going.

"Ouch, a sheriff killing another sheriff would be news, even in Florida."

"Yeah, so help me make sure it doesn't come to that."

"Let me check my email. I sent a couple of requests off earlier today. Looks like I got answers to most of them. I'll call you back in ten."

While we waited, we took Mauser out for a walk. The big dog was good therapy for all of us. Pete called as we were heading back to the house.

"Your boy Owen has some debt. About seventy thousand in student loans, thirty in credit cards and he bought a house last year with a half-million-dollar price tag. Since then, he's missed a few student loan and credit card payments. You said he'd inherit a healthy sum. Bingo, I'd say you have a solid motive. I looked into his mother's finances too, but I swear rich people are harder to read. She doesn't have any debt, but I've got no clue as to her net worth except that she owns a number of properties, all mortgage free. I'd say she was in good shape."

"Could you tell what Owen spends his money on?"

"Well, he made a trip to Jacksonville six months ago."

"Okay, you buried the lead there, big guy."

"If I get the time, I'll check and see if he got a rental car and what the mileage was," Pete said, anticipating my next request.

"What about the Leonards?"

"They are in much better shape than Lampert. No question there. But they *did* take out a second mortgage on their house last year. They've got some credit card debt too, looks like about twenty-five thousand. Without a warrant, you aren't going to get much deeper into their finances."

"Klein?"

"That dude owns a lot of property. Buys and sells like no man's business. He's also filed a number of lawsuits and been named in a number of lawsuits. He's been in litigation with at least a dozen people within five miles of where he lives. He must be a real jackass. But other than having a team of lawyers on a short leash, he doesn't have any red flags. Oh, he was a victim in an assault case. Apparently some guy punched him out. I read the report. Sounds like the prosecutor could have charged Klein's attacker with attempted murder, but instead just went for assault. Which is odd, since prosecutors normally like to go for the jugular and then plead down. Hold on, Charles Vargas was the prosecutor on that one. I've worked with him before. Let me put you on hold. I might get lucky and catch him in the office."

I tried to tell Pete to just call me back, but before I could say anything he was already gone.

"You there?" he asked, coming back on the line a few minutes later.

"Yeah, what's the word?"

"I got lucky. You'll love this. Vargas said that after he met with Klein, *he* wanted to punch the guy's lights out, so he thought it would be hypocritical of him to push the charges up. At one point, Klein actually threatened to sue the prosecutor. Vargas said he felt like he was prosecuting the wrong man, and it was the first time he ever apologized to a defendant."

"Ha! That all?"

"That's what I could get sitting on my butt up here. You're on the ground," Pete said encouragingly.

"I'll keep you updated. Unless something dramatic happens, I'll be back at work on Wednesday."

"Hey, no one else cares, but Darlene and I miss you."

"Thanks, buddy."

Hanging up, I turned to Dad and Sullivan, who'd been listening to my end of the conversation. "We might want to take a closer look at Owen. The man's been on the rocks with his finances, and he also forgot to mention that he was in Florida a few months ago."

"Jacksonville is only about four hours from here," Sullivan said.

"You really think he could have hired someone to kill his mother?" Dad asked.

"He was sure on the plane headed down here fast," I said. "And money talks."

"He hires a killer who stalks his mother for a couple of weeks. She's feeling like someone is following her, so she hires Fowler. Fowler gets murdered by the hired killer, who then murders the mother as per the contract. Okay, that's fine as far as it goes, but how does that explain the Fernandezes?" Dad frowned.

"Maybe he scoped out the Fernandezes and noticed that they had a lot of money, so he figured he'd get a little extra gravy," Sullivan suggested.

"There are rich people all over this island. Why the Fernandezes?" Dad pressed.

"Good question," I admitted. "It would make more sense if they were good friends with Pauline."

"No one has put them together," Sullivan said. "They might have met at some island social functions, but there was a pretty big age difference between the couple and Pauline. I've noticed with these rich folk that they tend to sort out by age."

"I agree," Dad said.

"Could they have seen something?" I asked.

"Possibly. Maybe the killer noticed them looking at his car. He thought they might have written down his number, so he decided to ask them a few questions and then make sure that they couldn't ever answer questions again."

"Oh, that reminds me. Yeah, yeah, that could be what happened. Because Ralph Fernandez's hand was smashed pretty good. And a finger on his other hand was broken," Sullivan told us excitedly.

"A little bit of torture would fit in with your theory." Dad nodded. "He wanted to make sure that they hadn't already passed on the information. He does some improvisation with the butt of a gun, Fernandez tells him what he wants, including the combo to the safe, and then our guy offs him."

"And he doesn't worry about the torture because it fits in with his scenario of a burglar torturing the homeowner to get the combination to the safe."

"Fits pretty nice," Sullivan said.

"When I first became a deputy, a prosecutor told me that he always loved it when the motive of a murder was sex or money, because they were easy for the jury to understand.

No complicated flow charts or getting into the head of a crazy person. Just normal, everyday motivations. Every juror has been motivated by sex or money, so you don't even have to explain it to them," I said.

"He has a point," Dad agreed.

"We need to put some pressure on—" My phone rang and I looked at the number. "Speak of the devil," I said and answered it. "Mr. Lampert." I almost said, "We were just talking about you," but I thought better of it and said instead, "What can I do for you?"

"You said to call you if I came across anything strange in my mother's house. Well, I have."

I thought about asking what it was, but I decided that this would provide a perfect opportunity to talk to him when he had initiated the contact. "Look, I was just heading out," I lied. "Why don't I stop by and you can show me whatever it is?"

"That would be great. It's kind of hard to explain anyway."

"I'll be there shortly." I disconnected and turned to the others. "If all of us go, we're liable to spook him."

"You go," Dad said. "He made contact with you, so we'll roll with that. Maybe this is a classic case of the bad guy wanting to be close to the investigation."

"We'll see what he has to show me. That'll tell us a lot."

"True. If he's just making stuff up, then you'll know that he wanted to find out what's going on with the investigation. I've heard that killers often do that," Sullivan mused.

"That's why the Leonards are of interest. Killers often pretend to discover the body so that they'll be embedded into the investigation from the start. Others come up with false leads or fake evidence. Both to throw the investigators off of the scent and to be close to the case," Dad explained. "You better get going," he said to me.

CHAPTER NINETEEN

Red flags started flying as soon as I walked into Pauline's house. Owen had clearly spent the day tagging and cataloging items around the house. There must have been a hundred sticky notes in the living room alone. It looked like he was identifying each item and then assigning it a possible value. Who does that the day after their mother's suicide?

"I guess this looks odd," he tried to explain. "I'm a bit OCD, which is what makes me such a good researcher and historian. Also, I couldn't sleep last night. I've got some late summer classes that start in two weeks. I'd like to get the estate settled by then. You think I'm pretty cold, right?"

"I'm not here to judge," I said, judging that he was one cold fish.

"I hated my mother for over a decade. Emotionally, I just can't make a U-turn and start weeping because she's dead." Was he trying to get my approval? Or maybe just my understanding?

"Seriously, I've been in law enforcement long enough that I've seen all kinds of reactions to death. Yours is not the strangest." *Maybe the most hard-hearted*, I thought.

"Let me show you what I found. This is going to seem odd too. But I worked my way through college as a home inspector. My OCD paying off again. So I know what to look for in a house." He was walking over to the wall where there was a small stepladder. He climbed up on it and pointed to a spot where the crown molding came together.

"Do you see it?"

I peered at the spot he was pointing to. Maybe there was something there, but I sure couldn't see it. "Honestly? No."

"Here, get up on the ladder." He climbed down.

Once on the ladder, I could see that there was a little hole about the size of a pencil eraser. It was nothing. I lived in a mobile home. There were cracks and gaps everywhere. Who knew what had caused it, but I didn't think it was a big clue in a murder case.

"I see what you're talking about," I said noncommittally. "I'm just not sure how important it is."

"Okay. But I've found a couple more just like it. One in the bedroom and another in the office." His voice was excited.

This guy is nuts, I thought. Maybe the OCD was taking over. Aloud, I said, "Yeah, still…" I stalled, not wanting to be too negative. I still had my own agenda for this meeting.

"Okay, okay, come into the kitchen then." He was pretty wired. I wondered if he'd been downing energy drinks while he wasn't sleeping. Or maybe there were some meds he should have been taking.

I followed him into the kitchen, where he went down on his knees and peered up at the bottom of the cabinets above the counters. He twisted his head right, left and then right again.

"Squat down," he instructed.

Hesitantly, I got down on my knees.

"There and there," he said, pointing to the underside of the cabinets. Again, I could see some small holes, but I had no idea if they were a normal part of cabinet construction or not. I tried to think what the underside of my cabinets looked like. I was pretty sure that they were unfinished and they probably had holes all over them. I remembered repairing the track in one of my kitchen drawers last year and being shocked at how sloppy some of the work was. There had been places where screws weren't tightened down and other places where they hadn't even bothered to put in a screw. *Speaking of loose screws*, I thought.

"I see what you mean," I lied. "Interesting." No, it wasn't. I got up off of the floor.

"There are places like that in the bathrooms too."

"Mmmm," I said and I hoped it sounded thoughtful. "That's very curious. I appreciate you telling me about this."

"I'm not sure what it means," he said. "I just know that, in a house like this, they shouldn't be there. When I first saw them I thought they might be something a rodent or some other animal had done, but they're too perfect and symmetrical."

"I'd be curious about any theories you might come up with." This was true. I thought that hearing his theories would tell me a lot about him. Was he just strange, a little odd or a total paranoid schizophrenic? "While I'm here, I have a few questions I want to ask you."

"Sure." He was still thinking about his odd little holes.

I looked out the windows as though I was enjoying the view. "Florida in the summer. Wow. At least the water makes it a little more comfortable down here on the coast."

"And the storms," he said, nodding toward some dark clouds moving in off of the Gulf. It did look like we had the chance of a real storm this evening. Usually we'd get them every afternoon in the summer, but the weather had been dry so far this year.

"When was the last time that you were in Florida?" I asked casually.

"Funny, I was actually here last winter. St. Augustine for a history conference."

Okay, he got points for honesty.

"Must have been tough being in Florida, that physically close to your estranged mother. Did you think about coming over here?" I ventured, trying to sound innocent.

"No. But you're right, it was hard. Brought back a lot of memories." Even now I could hear the anger buried inside of him.

"She ever try to contact you?"

"No. I... No."

"What?"

"I'm not proud of what I did," he said morosely. *Elevator going down*, I thought. Bipolar? Manic depressive?

"What?" I encouraged. I wasn't going to go in for a hug, that's for sure.

"The last time I saw her was at my father's funeral. I told her what I suspected, and that I might go to the police. She called me a spoiled brat. Said that my father had needed my strength and I hadn't been there for him. All I could think of was seeing her with that other man. Whore, whore, whore! The word kept going around and around in my head. She stood there sneering at me. I could see my father's coffin standing open behind her and my hand just went back like it had a mind of its own. Next thing I knew, she was lying on the ground with the red mark of my palm across her face. I ran from the funeral home and never talked to her again." He seemed drained of all the energy that had been coursing through him when I'd arrived at the house.

Part of me felt sorry for the man while another part thought that he was as crazy as a bed bug. Did this add up to a man who would hire a hitman? What I'd seen was pushing me toward the *yes* column. He appeared to be in a downward spiral.

"Come on, sit down." I guided him over to the couch. "Can I get you something to drink? Maybe a little brandy?" Wasn't brandy what they gave to hysterical people in those old black-and-white movies?

"No. Alcohol... does things to me," he said and I involuntarily rolled my eyes. How many issues could one guy have?

"Water, at least."

"Sure. She has some bottles of water in the refrigerator."

He lay back on the couch and closed his eyes.

What have I gotten myself into? I thought. Telling myself that I'd better take advantage of the situation, I brought him the water. He drank about half the bottle before sitting back up and opening his eyes.

"I guess you must think I'm crazy?"

Absolutely, I thought. Aloud, I said, "No, not at all. Like I said, I've seen a lot of people at their best and worst during my time as a deputy."

I let him drink a bit more water, then said, "St. Augustine is a fascinating town. Cara, my girlfriend, and I have talked about going over there for a weekend getaway. First time I went was with my mom and dad. I was probably ten. The fort absolutely fascinated me." I wanted to pry out some more info on his trip. Dates, length of stay… anything I could get.

"Oldest European settled city in North America. I had a great trip. In fact, the only cloud over it was knowing that I was in the same state as my mother." He proceeded to bang his head with his fists. "I'm an idiot."

"You said you were there for a conference?" I said, trying to guide him back on track.

"Yeah, the Colonial Historians Association."

"Didn't you say your area of interest is twentieth-century America?"

"I was thinking of spreading my wings a bit. I've had to cover general survey classes in American history for a few semesters. I thought I ought to expand my knowledge base. Honestly, I'm bucking for dean, so having broader interests is a good thing. At least that's what a friend of mine advised. Bastard is already an assistant dean at an Ivy League school. Not Harvard or Yale." Owen was rambling like he was drunk. I wondered again if there were some prescription narcotics that he should have been taking.

"First time in St. Augustine?"

"The old city is amazing. Pretty well done. Shame they lost a lot of it before they realized what a tourist attraction it could be. Historical preservation is like wilderness conservation. It has to attract users in order to be preserved, but the tourists or loggers or hunters end up damaging what they're trying to save. A paradox. Oh, shit, I just need to get some sleep." He fell over, resting against the arm of the couch with the half full bottle of water precariously held in his hand.

"How long did you stay?"

"What, at the conference? I don't know. Five days, about. Ugggh." His eyes fluttered closed and I decided that I'd gotten all I was going to get.

"I'll let you get some rest."

As soon as I said this, his head popped up. "You're going to look into those holes?" he asked, looking at me expectantly.

"I will," I assured him with my fingers crossed behind my back and quickly made my way out.

When I got back to the house, Dad and Sullivan were sharing the couch with Mauser and watching the TV intently, as if it was playing a mashup of the Super Bowl, the World Series and the Final Four.

"Come see this," Dad said with a rabid intensity that told me he'd found some red meat.

Sitting down beside him, I immediately recognized what they were watching. On the screen was the image of a room shot from a downward angle. Three men were on screen. Jerome sat in a chair beside a small table. His right hand was handcuffed to a ring attached to the table. He was moving his head around in a rhythmic back-and-forth motion. Sitting in front of him, almost between his legs, was Sheriff Duncan, while another deputy paced around the room behind him.

I watched the video for ten minutes and felt sick. The amount of coercion that Duncan was using was excessive. I didn't know how far into the interrogation process the scenes I was watching were, but it was clear that Jerome had already been broken. Whatever the sheriff said, Jerome was willing to repeat.

They were going over the details of how Fowler's murder had gone down, or at least Duncan's version of it. He got Jerome to say that he'd hit Fowler on the back of the head with a pipe. With Fowler unconscious, Jerome agreed that he'd put Fowler into an old boat on Fowler's property. There was bilge water in the bottom of the boat and Fowler had gagged and choked. Worried that Fowler would be mad if he woke up, Jerome said he held his head in the water until he'd drowned. Afterward, he had driven the body down to the coast and dumped it in the Gulf.

"What an asshole," I said, watching Duncan manipulate Jerome by promising to take him home, telling him that anyone might have done the same thing, and not to worry because he was Jerome's friend. All he had to do was sign a statement and everything would be fine. Duncan used all of the classic techniques to get a false confession. "You can tell the investigator in there with him isn't happy."

"No. He started the interview and, after about fifteen minutes, Duncan charged in and took over," Dad said.

"Where'd you get this?" I asked.

"Somebody Sullivan knows."

"Quinn got it from someone and passed it on to me." Sullivan looked up from the TV.

"How does Duncan think he's going to get away with this?"

"There are parts of the interrogation where Duncan reverts to something close to a professional attitude. My guess is that Duncan plans to edit the tape. He should be able to get about ten minutes where he's just asking questions and Jerome is answering with the information that Duncan crammed down his throat earlier."

"But wouldn't there be time gaps?"

Dad shrugged. "With the editing equipment available today, who knows? Edit the video. Zoom in so that the original time stamp doesn't show, and then rerecord the edited footage with another camera to put a new and continuous time stamp on it. Or he might just go with the quick and dirty excuse that the camera was malfunctioning, we lost the footage or whatever. Once the prosecutor has the confession in front of the jury, it'll pretty much be game over. Juries want to believe confessions."

I knew that this was true. Juries would ignore a lot of misconduct or incompetence if they viewed an accused person's confession.

"What are you going to do with this?" I asked.

"That's the question of the hour. If we give it to Jay, it will take a while before it will do Jerome any good. Also, it would be subject to a lot of investigation and disclosure, which none of us would want," Sullivan said.

"We're in luck. I know a guy," I told them, pulling out my phone. I had to hunt for a copy of *The Pelican Brief* to get Luke Garner's number.

When Dad saw the paper, he smiled. "That'll work."

CHAPTER TWENTY

Once Luke Garner was standing in our living room, I started my lecture.

"Ground rules." I held up a finger. "Number one is that this gets out fast and with the right slant. Number two," I held up another finger, "no one knows how you got this." A third finger went up. "Number three is, don't forget number two."

"Yeah, yeah, cool, I got it."

We sat him down and showed him the video. He asked a few questions, but for the most part he watched it silently, shaking his head sadly from time to time.

"Wow! I kinda knew that Duncan was an ass, but I figured that went with being a sheriff." He turned to Dad. "No offense."

"None taken," Dad assured him. "But there's a difference between being a bit of a hard-ass and being unprofessional, or even criminal. What you've seen is criminal activity. Duncan is purposely violating Jerome's civil rights."

"So why don't you take it to FDLE or the Feds and let them investigate?"

"Jerome has already been affected by Duncan's actions. I think the sooner we can get him out of jail, the better. By releasing this through the media, Duncan might be able to avoid a full investigation, but I think he's going to get a lot of pressure from the State Attorney to cut Jerome loose."

"I can see that," Luke said thoughtfully. "I got a friend at the TV station in Panama City. They love this kind of stuff."

"Will they protect their sources?"

"Hell, yeah! Besides, they'll just know it's coming from me, and I ain't telling."

"Good enough for me," Sullivan said.

We gave Luke a copy of the video and I could tell that he was already envisioning himself as another Woodward or Bernstein. "My only question is, what cool nickname should I have?" he said as I handed him the footage.

"I'd avoid all the ones that have a pornographic undertone. Deep Throat always made me feel kind of icky."

"Yeah, but you remember it, don't you?" he said, tapping the flash drive against his forehead.

Sullivan asked Sally to bring over barbeque for dinner. We didn't tell her about the interview footage. We'd agreed that the fewer people who knew about it, the better. This included leaving Cara and Genie in the dark, but it was best that way. Loose lips sink ships.

"Did you find out anything from Owen?" Dad asked as we sorted through the bags of pulled pork sandwiches and sides.

"That was an interesting experience. He's got issues that make him a more viable suspect." I filled them in on the rather odd visit.

"Guy sounds like a nut," Sally summed up.

"He came across like a nut," I agreed. "But taking into account the life he's had and the last forty-eight hours, maybe his emotional breakdown is somewhat understandable."

"He hit his mother at his father's funeral." Sullivan shook his head. "For me, that's unimaginable. A guy who would do that..."

"I don't disagree." I bit into my sandwich and

remembered how hungry I was.

"He's on the top of my list," Sally added.

"I'd like it better if he did it directly. Competent hired hitmen are characters out of the movies. The reality is that you get some morons that make a million mistakes and land everyone in jail. What our crime scenes reflect is someone who's in control and knows what they're doing," Dad said.

"Like someone with OCD." I tried to clean the barbeque sauce from my hands and face.

"You have to get him down here from New York and back," Dad said.

"Not possible." Sally said. "I checked with the airline. He was on the flight from New York and he hasn't taken any other flights in the last two weeks."

"Private plane?" I offered.

"If you can prove it, I'd believe it," Dad said.

"Coming down here, committing the murders, flying back up there and then coming back down here would certainly explain his near-total exhaustion."

"Simple enough to prove. Don't forget that he was supposed to be at family wedding. Ask him for contact numbers and check them out. Five or six hours is probably the minimum travel time from his place in New York to here using a private plane. Plus, he'd have to get a car when he was here," Dad said.

I held up my hands in surrender. "I get it. One or two checks and I'll give it up. But there is still the possibility of the hitman. Good hitmen probably *do* exist outside of the mafia," I said. Dad just raised his eyebrows.

We talked about the Leonards for a while. The biggest question with them was what they would have had to gain. No one had a good answer.

"Tomorrow I want to go see Jerome," Dad said.

"I'll go with you," I said. "I'd like to check out the property records for some of our suspects and see if there are any red flags. I'll go by the zoning office too, follow up on Owen's paranoid fantasies. Would be interesting if all the houses used the same builder."

"Maybe the houses are substandard or something. They could be toxic. I heard about a case where the houses had this strange black mold that was literally killing people. A high-end builder might be willing to kill to keep it a secret," Sally said.

"There were all those toxic FEMA trailers after Katrina," Sullivan reminded her. He turned to us. "While you're on the mainland, why don't you check up on Klein's alibi? The not-so-mysterious Judith and her commissioner husband live up there. She works at a dress shop not far from the courthouse."

We devised an action plan for Tuesday that included Sullivan finding out what he could about the Fernandezes' autopsies and the crime scene tech reports. Sally was going to talk to as many locals as possible and see if she could make any more connections between the victims and our list of material witnesses.

After the company left, I called and talked to Cara, filling her in on what I could.

"I brought home some of the puzzle," she told me.

"Good. We haven't had any time to work on it."

"I haven't had much luck. Ivy's having a good time with it, though. I do think she misses you."

"Tell her I miss all of her annoying cat habits too," I said good-naturedly. "How's Alvin?"

"Sleeping, glad to be home."

"I'll be glad to be home too. Not what I envisioned when I thought about taking a vacation."

"Do you think you'll be able to accomplish anything tomorrow?"

"I think…" I almost told her that I thought we might have secured Jerome's release, but since the station hadn't yet done their report on Jerome's coerced confession, that would have been showing our hand. "I *hope* we'll get a break," I finished lamely.

We talked a bit longer and then I got ready for bed. Since

Cara wasn't there, I decided to leave my door open so that the air conditioning would circulate a little better. I wasn't thinking. I woke an hour later when a lumbering bear climbed into my bed. It took me a moment and the scent of dog to recognize that my new bed companion was Mauser. We fought over the bed and the covers for a while before he agreed to take seventy percent and leave me thirty of each.

I was dreaming that I was standing on a train platform, watching a locomotive as it started out of the station. The huffing of the engine was loud and water from the steam engines began to drip on me. That's when I woke up to find Mauser standing over me, drooling and chuffing at the window. This sort of behavior usually meant that there was some sort of annoying sound that was bothering him. I told him it was nothing, but he wouldn't settle down. I listened. Still nothing but more huffing from Mauser, punctuated by a soft, deep-throated bark.

Irritated, I got out of bed and went over to the window he was focused on. It looked out over the Leonards' property. I could see lights on next door. I opened the sliding glass door and stepped out onto the balcony, then I finally I heard what he'd heard. That sound of a boat motor idling.

From the balcony, my view of their house was blocked by a tree. I looked at my watch. Three in the morning seemed a little early, even to be going fishing. I went back inside and put on my shorts and a T-shirt.

"Damn you, dog," I told Mauser, who'd flopped over to steal my part of the bed too. "Oh, now you can live with the noise. Great."

I grabbed a flashlight and my gun before leaving the house.

There was enough moon to see where I was going, which was good. I didn't want to use the flashlight if I didn't have to. In full Peeping Tom mode, I crept around the house, trying to use the shrubbery as cover. I could get within seventy-five feet of the boat dock without exposing myself.

What I witnessed was enough to drive a sane lawman crazy. The Leonards were carrying boxes to their boat. I could just make out what they were saying from my position crouched behind a bunch of oleanders.

"I think you're overreacting," Courtney said.

"Right. I bet you'll cut a deal at the first opportunity," Bob hissed back at her.

A deal for what? I knew what it sounded like, but misinterpretations are possible. Besides, even if they were talking about illegal activity, I didn't have probable cause to do anything.

"This is crazy."

"Keeping this stuff was crazy."

"But…" Courtney stopped. "I just want this all to be over."

"Then quit talking and help me get everything loaded up."

"Bob?"

"What?" he said, exasperated.

"I'm really scared."

"Me too. That's why I'm getting rid of this stuff."

"Not that. Him."

"That too. After the body, who wouldn't be scared?"

"Can I go with you?"

"Now?"

"Please?"

"Is this the last of them?"

"Yes."

"If you're ready, then let's go," Bob told her, and in seconds they were on the boat.

There was nothing I could do as I watched the boat move away from the dock. Even if I'd tried some sort of Schwarzenegger-run-and-jump-on-the-boat move, Bob could have gunned the engines and left me swimming in the Gulf. And what justification would I have had if something went tragically wrong? A half heard conversation and vague suspicions?

In the end, all I could do was stand up and watch the white wake of their boat moving farther and farther away. Feeling frustrated and angry at myself for doing the only thing I could, I headed back to the battle for the bed.

I woke up with the sun and couldn't get back to sleep. My mind was racing through all sorts of scenarios and trying to come up with answers when it didn't have nearly enough information. I finally gave up and grabbed my phone, seeing that it was a few minutes after seven o'clock. There was a message from Cara.

Opening it, I read: *Bingo! Found a note that includes Fowler's name!! Also a list of addresses. Looks like Pauline was taking notes. Love you! Got to go to bed and get at least a couple hours sleep. See you tomorrow.* Following this text was a list of addresses. I scanned them, but didn't recognize any. I looked at the time on the messages. Cara had sent them at four in the morning. Crazy woman. But having more evidence confirming the ties between Fowler and Schultz was great, even if I didn't know where it was going to lead.

I took Mauser for an early walk, which included looking at the Leonards' dock. The boat was back in the davits as though nothing had happened.

Back in the house and eating a balanced breakfast of leftover coleslaw, I recounted the previous night's adventures to Dad.

"Good boy," he told Mauser, who accepted a hearty petting. I got, "Are you sure they were carrying boxes?"

"Yes, and I heard what I heard," I said, letting my frustration with the situation boil over into a more general irritation. "Whatever evidence they had in that house is gone now."

"Could be related to something else," he said.

"You don't believe that."

"No. But there wasn't anything you could do to stop them, so you might as well let it go. We can use that later if we have to question them again. We interject it at the right moment, it might rattle them to know that they were seen." He was right, of course. I nodded.

I opened my laptop, scanned social media and checked out the local news to make sure the interrogation footage hadn't gotten out yet. I did discover something interesting about Ralph Fernandez.

"Listen to this," I told Dad, who was drinking coffee and answering emails and messages.

"The headline reads: *Murdered Man is Illegal Immigrant. Forty-five-year-old Ralph Fernandez, who was killed over the weekend on Pelican Island, has been identified as Victor Rodriguez, an El Salvadorian national who had been deported several times in the 1980s. The murdered man's picture was recognized by former friends of Victor Rodriguez. Rodriguez had been presumed lost in the desert on the U.S.-Mexico border.*" I stopped and looked at Dad, who was listening intently.

"That's a bit of a surprise."

"There's more, but it's mostly just emotional anecdotes from friends of both Fernandez and his alter ego. Great, we have another weird factor to fit into our equation."

"Don't use math metaphors. You were awful when it came to math."

"It was the lack of parental support," I said and finished my coleslaw.

An hour later we were sitting in front of the jail on the mainland.

"Do you want me to come in?" I was worried what would happen if sheriff matter met sheriff anti-matter.

"No. If I'm lucky, Duncan won't be here. Besides, Jay will be here to keep me out of trouble or to represent me if I get into trouble." Dad gave me a wicked smile. "I'll text you when I'm done."

At the courthouse, I found the property appraiser's office easily enough. I gave a brief explanation of why I was there that included a quick flash of my badge. Not that I was trying to imply that I was with the local sheriff's office, but a little badge can go a long way. I also handed over the freshly made donuts that I'd gotten from a bakery Sally had recommended. I showed them my list and they gladly retrieved the portfolios I needed as they munched happily on chocolate cream pastries.

Next I made a stop for a bucket of chicken and headed over to the zoning department. The files from the property appraiser had revealed that all of the homes *had* been built by the same builder.

I stopped a guy wearing a name tag that read: *Building Inspector Ross Newton.* I gave him the quick badge flash and offered him some chicken. "Hi. I wondered if I could talk to you about some of the homes out on Pelican Island?"

"Sure, what do you need to know?"

"I was looking into some homeowners on the island and noticed that all of their homes were built by the same construction company. Is that the norm?"

"I'm not surprised. There are only a couple of high-end builders in the area. And usually, if a company is working in an area, it's good advertising. Other people who have bought lots will stop and talk to them and, next thing you know, there's a whole cluster of new homes being built by one company." He tore the meat off of a leg.

"Did you inspect the houses on the island?"

"Which ones? When were they built? I worked out there a few years ago. Now I'm doing all the area within two miles of town."

"Most of the ones I'm looking at were built between ten and five years ago."

"Sounds about right."

"What if I told you there were holes in the molding? Like up at the corner where the molding comes together," I said, pointing to the corner of the ceiling in the office. I felt like the guy who listens to a conspiracy podcast and is suddenly trying to convince everyone to put on tinfoil hats.

"I'd say call Roger's Pest Control. We're in the subtropics. We've got an alphabet soup of wood-boring insects." He tossed a cleared off breast bone in the garbage and wiped his fingers clean.

"Thanks."

I'd done my duty by Owen and presented his problem to an expert. He could get someone from a pest control company to look at it if he wanted to. One problem solved.

CHAPTER TWENTY-ONE

Dad texted me from the jail. I picked him up and let him drive so that I could navigate to Judith's store.

"It was rough. Jerome's not doing well. I was tempted to tell him and Jay about the leaked footage, just to make him feel better," Dad said.

"With luck, he won't have to be in there much longer," I consoled him.

"Horrible to think that, without a whistleblower, he might have to be in jail for months or even a year until his trial."

"Having a good sheriff means a lot for a county."

"Even if I lose in November, we'll still have a better sheriff. Maxwell's full of himself, but he'd never stoop as low as Duncan," Dad said and I had to agree. It was a cheap shot that Chief Maxwell had decided to run against Dad for sheriff. However, as pompous as Maxwell was, he did conduct himself like a professional law enforcement officer whose goal was to keep good folks safe and put bad guys in jail.

"There's the store," I said, pointing to a small boutique that looked out of place. The county seat was twenty miles from the coast, pretty far removed from the more touristy and upscale parts of the county where such stores tended to congregate. But maybe Judith was good with the books or had a reputation that drew people to her store.

There was one customer inside when we came in. She was holding up a dress and talking with the dark-haired woman behind the counter. Both of them stopped what they were doing and turned to look at us like we were Martians.

"Can I help you?" the woman behind the counter asked. It was clear that she thought we were lost.

"Are you Judith Murray?" Dad asked, honey-tongued.

"I am."

"When you get the chance, we'd like to ask you a couple of questions."

Her expression darkened, as though she already knew why we were there.

"I see. If you'll wait, I'll be right with you," she said curtly.

In a few minutes a credit card had been run and the dress bagged up for the customer, who gave us a sideways look on her way out.

"What are your questions?" Judith flung at us.

"I'm Sheriff Macklin and this is Deputy Macklin. We're from Adams County."

"You aren't the sheriff here."

"Like I said, I'm the sheriff in Adams County. We're assisting Chief Sullivan from Pelican Island." Dad spoke slowly and calmly.

"Do you know who my husband is?"

"He's a county commissioner."

"Yes, that's right."

"Do you know Blake Klein?"

"Maybe," she said suspiciously. She was the worst type of subject to interview. You had to pry every word out of them like you were taking acorns from a squirrel.

"Mrs. Murray, if what we've heard about your relationship with Mr. Klein is true, then I doubt that you want to answer these questions in a more formal or public manner." Dad sounded like he was part funeral director and part FBI agent.

"I know him."

"Do you have a romantic relationship with him?"

"I thought it was romantic. Apparently he thought it was friends with benefits," she snapped.

"When did you last see him?"

"Saturday afternoon."

Dad and I looked at each other. Her sudden candor was a surprise. All we'd been hoping to do was establish whether Klein had been telling the truth about his relationship with her. Now she was admitting to being with him on the day of the shooting.

"Where?"

"At his place."

"Tell us about that meeting."

"*He* was there," she said, glancing at me with hard, cold eyes. Eyes that I could imagine sighting down a barrel to take pot-shots at an ex. "That's all I'm going to say. Ask any more questions and I'll get my lawyer to talk with you."

Dad looked at her curiously. "Just one more question," he said, holding up his finger. "Answer it and I promise we'll leave."

"No."

"I'm going to write a couple of things down on this piece of paper," Dad said, taking a notepad out of his pocket. "You just point to the right one. I won't even let him see it. Then it would all be just I-said-you-said if it ever got to court. There'll be no chance that you're incriminating yourself."

I stayed where I was as he stepped up to the counter and wrote something on the pad, then showed it to the angry woman.

"You understand what I've written?"

"I understand."

Tentatively, her finger went out toward the paper, then suddenly she jabbed at it.

"Now get out. Get out!" Her voice was perilously close to a scream.

Dad turned and headed for the door, but I beat him to it. I didn't want to be the last one out of there.

As we walked to the car he showed me the paper. He'd written: *.45, .22, .38, .50, 9mm.*

"Which one did she point to?"

"The .38."

Dad called Sullivan, who put him on hold to call Sally, who reported that the lab had confirmed that the round collected at Klein's house had come from a .38.

"Well, that seems to clear that up," I said hesitantly.

"I don't know."

I sighed. "I know what you mean. Something about that whole encounter seemed wrong."

"Exactly. I don't know what bothered me most about it. The fact that she seemed to know who we were and why we were there, or the fact that she volunteered more information than she needed to."

"Maybe she just wanted it to be over with."

"Possibly."

"And she as much as said that she saw me there Saturday afternoon."

"But you didn't see *her.*"

"True."

On our way back to the island, we got a call from Jay Moreno.

"I'm sending you a link to a news segment that aired at noon today on a Panama City station. Watch it," he said and hung up.

We both knew what it was. I took Dad's phone and clicked on the link. A reporter talked about the video of the interrogation and used words that included *disturbing, abusive* and *coercive.* They interviewed a legal expert who said that, if what she'd seen was real, then the sheriff could face some difficult questions. It was a good, solid piece that was very sympathetic to Jerome and compared it to other recent cases where local law enforcement had used questionable tactics to get a confession.

I called Jay back and put him on speaker.

"What do ya think of that?" he asked, sounding like a kid who'd gotten a pony for his birthday.

"Terrific! How'd they get the video?" Dad said, winking at me.

"I don't know where they got a copy. My guess would be that Sheriff Duncan has made a few internal enemies over the years."

"That's not a surprise. What do you think Jerome's chances are now?"

"This morning, I'd have given him a two out of ten for being released before the trial and, even with my help, only a fifty-fifty shot at walking away from the trial a free man. Now, I'd give it a week and he'll be out. If not totally free, then at least released on bond."

"That's great news," I said. We all patted ourselves on the back and hung up.

"Obstruction of justice pays dividends sometimes," Dad said, a serious undertone to his voice. "I know that the end doesn't justify the means, but there are times when you just can't stay within the lines."

"We did the right thing."

"What's scary is, I agree with you."

We rode for a while in silence. I was trying to make sense of everything, but it was like trying to work a jigsaw puzzle that was missing pieces and without the box lid to refer to.

"Glue," Dad said suddenly.

"What?"

"We're missing the glue. We have the pieces, but nothing to hold them together."

"Funny. I was just thinking of the analogy of missing pieces from a jigsaw puzzle."

"Ha! I like mine better. I always think of the motive as the glue that holds the evidence together. What's the motive in this case?"

"Revenge and money if it's Owen. For anyone else, I have no idea."

"Great. We have one suspect who has several motives, but no opportunity, then we have plenty that have opportunity, but no motive."

"Owen hired someone. And it all makes more sense without that stupid shooting."

"Yeah, it lays out pretty well if you can get Owen to have hired a hitman."

"How hard can it be?" I said facetiously.

"The Leonards found the first body, and they seem to be involved in something underhanded. Who found the second body?" Dad answered his own question before I could say anything. "Dispatch got a couple of calls at almost the same time, which is understandable since she was flapping in the wind for everyone to see."

I cleared my throat.

"Too soon?" he asked.

"It's a little rough on the old woman."

"If you believe her son, she's a serial killer."

"I'm not sure I'm buying that. Yes, she might have... Probably *did* help them to commit suicide, but that's a grey area in a lot of people's books."

"Not the State of Florida's."

"True. So even if she did just assist in their suicides, she still committed a crime."

"A pretty serious crime. There are plenty of prosecutors who wouldn't hesitate to put her on trial for it."

"Okay, where were you going before I interrupted?"

"Damn it, I can't remember."

"Something about the Leonards discovering the body..."

"Oh, yeah. So the Leonards discovered the first body; the peanut gallery, the second; and the Holdens, the third and fourth. Rule one—always look closely at the person who finds a body."

"I see your point. But you talked to the Holdens."

"That was just preliminary, get-the-basic-facts-down

stuff. I think we ought to go at them a bit more aggressively."

"There's one big problem by the name of Duncan," I reminded him.

"He's going to be preoccupied with keeping his own ass away from the alligators for a while. We're just going to go talk to them as concerned citizens."

"I think you're playing with fire."

"Buck up. Let's go back to the house and walk Mauser, then we'll head for the Holdens." He was acting positively giddy now that the prospect of Jerome getting out of jail looked bright.

I got stuck taking Mauser out for his walk while Dad used the bathroom.

"Why don't you solve the crime?" I asked the beast as he sniffed every plant he came to. "Waking me up in the middle of the night when one pair of suspects is getting rid of evidence isn't that helpful if you don't have the paperwork allowing me to stop them."

Mauser ignored me, pulling me behind him from tree to tree. At least three of them received first class pee-mail to be read by the next dog that came by. "Can they tell how big you are from your scent?" I asked and received another tug in reply.

Dad had Mauser's lunch ready when we got back to the house.

"I think he's ready to go home," Dad said.

"Most be tough lying around a strange house all day," I said sarcastically.

"He's stressed," Dad assured me.

Mauser wolfed down his food and stumbled over to the couch. *What I'd give to be that stressed*, I thought.

"Dave bought this house from Wilkins," I tossed out idly.

"Did he?" Dad said, not really paying attention. He'd taken out his phone and was fielding emails. "There's going to be a bunch of work when we get back."

Most of the food that we'd brought for the trip was gone. I managed to find a bagel and smeared it with peanut butter for a passable lunch. As I ate, I called to check in with Sullivan, who'd spent the morning with Dr. Thomlinson going over the bodies of the Fernandezes.

"Nothing we didn't already know. The timeline is still between Saturday afternoon and Sunday morning."

"He couldn't narrow that window at all?"

"The house was cold and there certainly weren't any insects to help with determining the time," Sullivan explained.

"Okay, okay."

"We've got a couple of clean bullets if we ever find a gun to match them to. They don't match the bullet from the shooting," he said.

I didn't have high hopes for that. I was amazed whenever a murder weapon *was* found on the coast. With all of the water around, why wouldn't you just drop it in a deep spot and never think about it again? Of course, weapons that should have been lost are sometimes found in strange twists of serendipity.

"What about sexual assault?"

"Thomlinson doesn't think so. Hard to say since the couple was sexually active, but there wasn't any trauma or signs of recent activity."

"Sure is interesting about that video being released to the media," I said, sounding like a character in a comic book, but it's always better to be discreet than sorry.

"Yeah, I saw that. Hope it helps the guy," Sullivan said, with a clear wink-wink-nudge-nudge in his tone.

"The lawyer said he thought there was a very good chance of a positive outcome."

"Glad to hear it."

We hung up with promises to meet and compare notes later.

"Let's go see if we can find the Holdens."

Dad stood up, put his phone away and headed for the

door.

"Wait for me, Don Quixote," I said.

"Keep up, Sancho."

The truck was running by the time I got to it. The only thing scarier than Dad in a bad mood was Dad in a good mood.

"Shouldn't we have a plan of attack?"

"I don't know what I'm looking for."

"So it's one hundred percent fishing expedition?" I asked.

"Pretty much."

The Holdens let us in, which I thought was a little surprising. I guess Dad had made a good impression the first time he met with them.

"I appreciate you talking with us," he said as we sat down in their living room. The house had a cozy, lived-in feel. Normal and not as pretentious as most of the places on the island.

"We want to do all we can to help," Ed Holden said.

He was in his forties and would have been very good looking if he'd had more of a chin. Jessica Holden was sitting very close to her husband, holding his hand. Like a lot of couples that had lived together for a long time, they looked oddly similar, though, luckily for Jessica, she had a stronger chin.

"Sheriff Duncan was really angry when he found out you'd come by first and talked to us. I don't quite understand why you all aren't working together. But we know Chief Sullivan, and he said that you're a stand-up guy," Ed said.

"We saw that report on TV. We weren't happy with Duncan back when we were having all those burglaries out here. And now, seeing him browbeat that poor man…"

"We voted for the other guy in the last election," Ed said.

"We're not trying to stir anything up. Chief Sullivan asked for our help. We're just trying to do what we can," Dad told them.

"I wasn't here for any of the earlier interviews so, if you don't mind, we may cover some of the same ground you've already gone over," I said to get us started. "Tell me what happened from the moment you decided to go over to the Fernandezes' home."

"The man is like clockwork. He told me very specifically that he and Dana would be back on Sunday. I kept watch 'cause I really wanted his input on a stock I was going to buy. He got me started e-trading. Anyway, it was Monday morning and I knew I had to go knock on his door, see if I could tell what was going on."

"Did you go?" I asked Jessica.

She clutched her husband's hand tighter. "Yes. I thought it was a nice morning, I'd enjoy the walk." She shivered as she thought about discovering the bodies.

"Anyway, when we got there, no one answered the door. I decided to walk around the house. You know, make sure everything was okay. When I looked into the window of the garage door, I saw both cars, which was super weird. Ralph had said they were going to Destin. If they weren't home yet, then one of the cars should have been gone. None of it made sense. I should have called Chief Sullivan right then, but you don't think bad stuff is going to happen in your neighborhood. Right?"

"I told you I had a bad feeling. I mean, with that body that the Leonards found, and then poor Mrs. Schultz." Jessica half buried her face in Ed's shoulder. She looked to be roughly the same age as her husband, but there was a childish quality about her.

"So you kept checking out the house?" I prompted.

"That's right. When I got to the cottage door that leads into the garage, I saw the circle cut out of the glass." Ed stopped.

"You never should have gone in. I don't know why I let you," Jessica said.

He kissed the top of her head. "And I shouldn't have let you follow me in. Hindsight and all that," he apologized to her, then turned back to me.

"Was the door unlocked?"

"Absolutely. I tried the knob and it turned, so I pushed it open. I know it doesn't make much sense, but it was just like one action led to the next. Like my brain said the door is open so you have to go in. I'm in, so now I should check the house. I know how stupid it was."

"How did you go upstairs?"

"We used the elevator. I couldn't tell you where the stairs from the garage are. Anytime we've been over to their house, we've either gone up the outside steps to the front door or we've come in through the garage and ridden up in the elevator."

"So you took the elevator up…"

"Right. Looked around the kitchen. We both were yelling their names the whole time."

"Did you notice anything odd or out of place?"

"Oh, no. Dana always kept the house perfect. I'm embarrassed to admit it, but… No, it's stupid," Jessica said.

"Any thought you have might be important."

"Just… Okay, when we first started hanging out with them, I couldn't believe she kept the house like that. We have a maid come in twice a week and our place always looks… lived in. But Dana kept that place so neat that *Home and Garden* could have made a surprise visit and she would have been ready. At first I thought he must be really mean to make her work like that. I kind of saw him like one of those guys who will have a fit if something isn't just right."

Ed chuckled.

"What?"

"The irony is that it was Dana who insisted on the house being that clean. It was like she was afraid of something. Of course, we were shocked to find out he was… I guess you'd call him an illegal alien. Sounds so weird."

"Did you ever have any suspicions that Ralph wasn't who he said he was?" Dad asked.

"Never!" Ed said.

"Maybe that was it," Jessica said.

"What was it?" Dad asked.

"Maybe having to keep his secret all those years was what drove her. Keeping a secret bottled up for a long time can do some odd things to a person's psyche. The cleanliness might have been compensation. An outlet for her fears."

At that moment, Jessica and Ed exchanged a look. They locked eyes and an understanding passed between them. I was watching them when Ed broke it off and, as he turned his head away from his wife and saw me looking at him, I was surprised to see fear in his eyes.

Dad noticed that something was going on. Everyone was quiet for a moment. He looked back and forth at us until I nodded to let him know I'd explain later.

"What happened next?" I asked, trying to get the interview back on track, but the mood in the house had changed.

"I went into Ralph's office. He was lying there all covered in blood. We just turned and ran. I called 911 when we were back outside."

"You saw Ralph's body too?" I asked Jessica.

"Only for a second. I was following Ed and, when he saw the body, he turned and grabbed me. He hustled me out so fast. It was scary."

"I pretty much pushed her into the elevator. Look, that's really all we saw. I'd be glad to talk another time, but we've been overwhelmed by all this. I know you understand."

Ed stood up and walked us out. He was being very polite, but the bottom line was that he was pushing us out the door.

"What happened in there?" Dad asked as he opened the truck door.

"Something Jessica said, or the way she said it, got Ed upset. Or upset both of them. It was when she got all psychoanalytical about Mrs. Fernandez's house cleaning."

"You think house cleaning is a sore point with the Holdens?"

"No. I think the tension had to do with keeping a secret," I said as Dad started the truck. "Where are we going now?"

He sat there with the engine idling and the truck in park.

"I don't know." He sounded puzzled at his own indecision.

"It's almost time to feed your pet bear his late afternoon snack. Why don't we go back to the house? We'll lay everything out one more time and see if we can find any cracks that we can drive a wedge through."

CHAPTER TWENTY-TWO

We cleared the dining room table of the rest of Schultz's paper scraps so we could take Dad's notes and spread them out.

"We need to just go with our gut on some of this. Let's start at the beginning." He took the piece of paper that he'd written Claude Fowler's name on and placed it at one end. "Everything flows from here. So, question one: Did his body accidently wash up at the Leonards' place? I say no."

"I agree."

"Which means what?"

"That it was a message."

"Exactly, a message to the Leonards. But why to them? If Fowler was hired by Schultz, then why send a message to the Leonards?"

"They're involved somehow," I said.

"True. But they're victims, not the killer or one of his accomplices."

"That makes sense. So what were they getting rid of last night?"

"Something that would implicate the murderer? And Fowler's body was a warning that if they implicated him in whatever plot they're involved in, then he'd kill them too."

A. E. HOWE

"Okay."

"Just okay?" Dad asked.

"I don't know about the Leonards. I can't see those two in some grand plot. They're more like accidental bad guys."

"I know what you mean. People who might stumble into jail, but not the type to seek it out. Fine. Let's just say it was a warning and let it go at that."

"Perfect."

"Next, Pauline Schultz hears about the murder of Fowler and goes into action. Cleaning up her affairs and planning to take her own life."

"Or her death was the reason for everything else if we go with the son hires hitman scenario," I said, going back to my favorite theory.

"Let's look at that. If that's the case, then where do the Leonards fit in?"

"Good point. In that case we'd have to assume that the body washing up there was a coincidence that ratcheted up their paranoia about something else they were involved in, which caused them to get rid of something in the middle of the night. I don't like that. Too random."

"If the Leonards are involved, then your hired hitman theory definitely seems like a stretch."

"Maybe the Leonards *are* the hitmen. Somehow Owen meets them. They both have a mutual need for money. They agree to kill Schultz for Owen in exchange for part of the money he inherits." I was liking the idea, but then I came to a problem. "But why in the world would they drop Fowler off at their own dock? They have a perfectly good boat."

"That doesn't really work. You've got to drop the hitman angle," Dad told me.

I held up my hands in surrender. "Okay, I'll give it up. But he's still weird."

"So back to Schultz's suicide. I think, with the murderous son off the table, we can say that the odds are heavily in favor of suicide."

"Agreed. Why did she hire Fowler? And why did she kill

herself when he was murdered? Why not just go to the police?"

"If people don't go to the police, it's because they're scared or because they have something to hide," Dad said.

"She wasn't scared of dying, obviously. So that leaves something to hide. In fact, she might have hired Fowler to help her keep her secret. Looking at the shredded documents, I'd say she didn't want it to come out that she'd participated in her two husbands' suicides."

"Maybe she flat-out killed them?"

"Why, when we know they both were terminal? If someone had evidence that they could give to her son, who could then sue her for wrongful death, that could all be very ugly. Bad for her and bad for her son. I can see her doing anything to avoid the chance of a nuclear meltdown. If she kills herself, then the money goes to her son and he can move on."

"Good. I like that. Next would be the Fernandez murders."

"No. I want to put the shooting back in."

"Reasons?" Dad asked.

"Judith Murray was lying. I don't know about what or how much, but she was lying."

"She doesn't look like Klein's type. From the pictures in his house, he's more the blonde bombshell kind of rich guy. But he might have started the affair to have an inside track with a county commissioner. That wouldn't be a bad card for a real estate developer to have up his sleeve."

"I see that. But I can turn the argument around. If the affair with her was to have an inside card, why end the affair in a way that pisses everyone off? He would be jeopardizing his real estate dealings."

"Very good point. And he doesn't strike me as a man to go against his own interests. The shooting is back on the table," Dad agreed.

"Did she do it or didn't she?"

"Toss up." Dad shrugged.

"I think she knew we were coming. Klein must have called her and got her to agree to feed us that story."

"Which means he has something he can hold over her. She wasn't happy to spin that yarn."

"I see what you did there with the dress shop, spin that yarn."

"Thanks." He grinned.

"But you're right. So we have another person with a secret. I'm in the 'didn't do it' camp for Judith."

"Which begs the question of how she knew what caliber the gun was."

"Maybe a lucky guess."

"Possibly. One out of six odds that she'd guess the right one."

"Or Klein told her," I said slowly, feeling my eyes start to open.

Dad's phone rang. "Hey, Jay, what's up? Larry's here with me. I'll put you on speaker."

"Are you still down there on Pelican Island?" Jay asked.

"We're leaving in the morning. What's up?"

"I've been contacted by a dozen lawyers and families of people that Duncan has put in jail. This is going to go a lot deeper than our case. If I've gotten this many calls, then I'm sure there are a lot more."

"That's great," Dad said with a huge grin. I imagined that he was envisioning Duncan slow-roasting over a fire pit.

"It is, but I've got a friend who works at the jail down there, and when I talked to him he said the rumors going around the sheriff's office are that Duncan is on a rampage. He's talking about hunting down and arresting anyone and everyone involved in leaking that footage."

Dad's smile faded. "I see."

"So if you know of anyone who had a part in it," Jay said, his tone making it clear that he had a very good idea we were somehow involved, "I'd strongly suggest that they get out of the county until the dust settles. They also might want to warn any accomplices to do the same. The way this is building up, I would think that FDLE or maybe even the Feds will be involved soon. It already has the governor's attention."

"Thanks for the heads-up. If we run into anyone involved, we'll pass it along."

After Dad hung up, I gave Sullivan a call and told him what Jay had said.

"I'll keep my eye out and pass the warning along," he said, and I knew he meant he'd call Luke Garner.

"What do you think?" I asked Dad after hanging up.

"Duncan could be dangerous, sure. But odds are he'll just rant and rave. I'm not leaving until morning," he said, more out of stubbornness than discretion. "So where were we? The Fernandezes."

"You mean the Rodriquezes."

"That's right. More people with a secret," he said thoughtfully.

I remembered where my mind was going before Jay called. "They all have secrets. The Leonards, Pauline Schultz, Judith Murray and the Rodriquezes."

"Most people have secrets," Dad said, not trying to argue a point but rather thinking it through.

"Each of these folks seems to have a secret that they are willing to go to great lengths to keep hidden."

"Right." He looked at the names on the table. "And we suspect that Klein was using Judith's secret to force her to do his bidding. I'll even use the word blackmail."

"Could this all be about blackmail?"

"With Klein at the center of it. He sure is wealthy for being a rich man's underling," Dad said.

"If we're right, then the Leonards know what's going on," I said, looking in the direction of their house.

"Let's go have another talk with Bob."

We marched in lockstep to the Leonards' house. Dad thumped hard on the door.

"What do you want?" came Bob's voice from the other side.

"Open the door so we can talk!" Dad shouted back.

"You don't have no jurisdiction here. Go away."

"You don't want this to get ugly, Bob," Dad tossed back.

"If you don't get off my property, I'll call the sheriff."

"Bob, do you want us shouting your secret to everyone?" I yelled loudly enough for the neighbors to hear.

The door flew open. Dad gave me a smile.

"That's more friendly," Dad said and pushed his way into the house.

Bob was trying to look indignant, but came across more as confused. "I don't know what you're talking about," he stuttered.

"Way too late for that," I said.

"Get Courtney in here," Dad ordered.

"She's not feeling very well."

"Bullshit!" Dad barked.

"She was feeling well enough to help you dump boxes into the Gulf," I said and Bob's face went white.

He staggered over to the staircase. I thought for a moment he might have a stroke or a heart attack, but he managed to stay upright as he clung to the bannister.

"Courtney, get down here!" he yelled.

A few moments later, a contrite-looking Courtney came reluctantly down the stairs.

"Sit down," Dad told them when we were all standing in the living room. Both of them just fell back on the couch, never taking their eyes off of us.

"We are going to get to the bottom of this, so don't even think about stalling," Dad said, standing over them.

"We know that Klein was blackmailing you," I said.

Bob and Courtney looked at each other.

"It wasn't that bad," Bob said. "He told us what it would cost and we just had to pay him in cash every month."

"He told us to think of it as an additional homeowners' fee," Courtney said in a small voice.

"How long have you been paying him?"

"About five years. It started shortly after we bought this

house from him," Bob said.

"About three months afterward," Courtney added.

I tried to think of how to ask what their secret was. Bob thought we already knew. If he found out that we didn't, then he could just call Duncan. "What exactly were you getting rid of last night?" I finally asked.

"Stuff from our old life. Things we'd held onto even though we'd been warned about it," Bob said.

An old life? That didn't give me much to work with, but I forged ahead. Dad stayed quiet, letting me take the lead. "And when exactly did you break off from your old life?"

"1998, once the Feds convinced me to testify. They set us up in the witness protection program."

I tried to keep my mouth from falling open or exchanging looks with Dad. "So you kept stuff from your prior identity?"

"I know. They said we had to leave everything, but I snuck back and got a lot of stuff. Mostly sentimental things," Bob said.

"I begged him. It was my fault."

"We were on pretty rough ground marriage-wise, what with her finding out about my work with the Family. So I wanted to do whatever I could to keep her happy," Bob said, taking Courtney's hand.

"How sweet," Dad said sarcastically.

"I want to get the timetable down. You were contacted by the Feds and went into the witness protection program in 1998 and then testified that year."

"Right. I gave them everything they wanted in return for full immunity. Five members of the crime family running Seattle were convicted on my testimony."

"I was terrified," Courtney said.

"The Feds moved us around for a couple of years. Finally we settled down in Ohio. After that, we were able to pretty much live our lives like normal. I retired and we moved down here." Bob shrugged.

"But the Feds kept tabs on you?"

"Oh, yeah. And if we saw anything, I'd call and they'd come check it out."

"So you moved here and Klein started blackmailing you. How did he find out?"

"He came by a couple of times when we were moving in. I think he might have found one of our boxes with stuff from our other life," Bob said.

"Stupid of me to keep that stuff."

"I don't understand why you didn't tell your handlers?"

"We didn't want to go on the run again. And besides, Klein said he'd make sure the mob knew. Either way, our lives would be crazy again. I… We just didn't want to go through that. He came to us and we made a deal. If we paid him two thousand a month in cash, we'd be fine. Two thousand was worth it to us."

"Not easy financially, but worth it," Courtney said.

"Do you know why Pauline Schultz hired Claude Fowler?" I asked, switching tacks.

"No," Bob said adamantly. "First we heard about it was when Klein called us and said that if anyone else hired a private investigator, then the secrets would all go public. Honestly, that was the first time we found out that there were others."

"Who tried to kill Klein?"

"We don't know," they said in almost perfect unison.

We'd seemed to reach the end of the Leonards' involvement. They suspected that the Fernandez murders might be connected, but didn't have any direct knowledge. Convinced we'd gotten all we could, we headed back to our house.

Outside, the sun was starting to head for the horizon.

"What now?" I asked as we walked.

"Good question. In light of the situation with Duncan, I think we should pull our information together and get it to FDLE."

Back home, I took Mauser for a quick walk, then started to make him a snack of a Kong stuffed with peanut butter.

"Why am I taking care of your moose?" I yelled to Dad, who was standing at the dining room table.

"Because I'm thinking," he said distractedly. "I think that Ralph Fernandez took the shots at Klein and then Klein killed them in retaliation."

"Why?"

"The Leonards said that Klein called them and warned them after Fowler's body was found. Bob made it sound like he'd called everyone. That could have been the breaking point for the Fernandezes. So Ralph decides to issue a warning of his own to Klein."

With Mauser watching me intently, I set the jar of peanut butter down next to the Kong and turned to Dad. "I think you're right. But…"

I was interrupted by a loud crash caused by Mauser lunging for the Kong and knocking the glass jar of peanut butter to the floor. I whipped around as Mauser ran from the room with the Kong clamped in his jaws.

"You idiot, I haven't put the peanut butter in it. Don't complain to me. Look at the damn mess!" I yelled, eyeing the broken glass and peanut butter all over the kitchen floor.

"You should clean this up. He's your dog," I told Dad, who'd come over to see what had happened.

"You should have finished the Kong and given it to him before talking to me."

"You always take his side. Maybe if he knew how to wait, this wouldn't have happened," I grumbled, getting down on my knees to clean up the mess.

I started off by picking up the larger pieces of glass and setting them on the counter. I was lifting the last of the largest pieces when I noticed it—a little glint of light catching my eye. It was in the same spot as the holes that Owen had pointed out under Pauline Schultz's counters, but this wasn't a hole.

I looked closer. It was a little bubble of glass, about the size of the eraser on a pencil. The color of the glass matched the color of the cabinets almost perfectly. If there hadn't been a little bit of shine that caught the light, I wouldn't have noticed. I grabbed the butter knife and started to pry at the glass. After a couple minutes, I pulled out a device about the size of a AAA battery with wires running from it back into the cabinet.

My heart was racing now. I stood back up and looked at the ceiling, but there was nothing there. I ran into the living room, looking up into the corners of the ceiling. There was another one.

"What the hell is the matter with you?" Dad asked. "Hey, you can't leave that peanut butter on the floor. It has glass in it. Mauser will eat it!"

I ignored him, dragging a chair over to the living room wall and standing on it. The same kind of device was built into the molding at exactly the same spot where Owen had showed me the holes in his mother's house.

Dad, shaking his head and grumbling, had gone to clean up the peanut butter. I ran up to my bedroom and stood on another chair. Sure enough, there was another miniature camera mounted in the ceiling. I jumped down and ran down the stairs, my stomach tight with panic.

CHAPTER TWENTY-THREE

Dad was standing in the kitchen, staring at his phone. "Got a text from Sullivan. He said he just talked to Quinn and that nutcase Duncan has issued an arrest warrant for all of us." Dad sounded equal parts amused and disgusted.

"Let's take Mauser for a walk," I said emphatically.

"What are you talking about? Did you hear what I said?" Dad asked, looking at me like I'd gone crazy, which is probably exactly how it looked.

"I think Mauser's stomach is upset and he's going to have the runs," I said sternly.

"Oh, hell! Come on, let's get him outside!" Dad said, the arrest warrant forgotten. The threat of having to clean explosive Dane diarrhea from the interior of Dave's house was more than enough to get Dad focused and moving.

We dragged a confused Mauser out the door. Once we were in the yard and it was obvious that Mauser was fine, Dad gave me his *What the hell* look.

"He's not sick," I said once I'd judged we were far enough away from the house.

"What are you talking about? Have you gone mad?" Dad was confused and angry.

"The house is bugged," I said in a hoarse whisper.

"What?"

"That's how Klein knows everyone's secrets. He preinstalls electronic monitoring cameras and microphones in all the houses he sells," I explained.

Dad's face went blank. "Son of a bitch."

"We've been talking about going to FDLE," I told him. "He probably already knows that we know."

Before Dad could say anything else, we heard the sirens.

"That could be Duncan's men coming for us," Dad muttered.

"We can't risk being caught right now. We don't know who else Klein is able to manipulate."

"And Duncan isn't going to listen to our harebrained ideas of blackmail."

"Exactly."

"Only one road off the island."

"He'll have it blocked. That's why he's free to use his sirens."

"Joke's on him. We'll take Dave's boat," Dad said.

We started running toward the dock. Unfortunately, I had a hundred-and-ninety-pound weight on the end of a leash who didn't want to go for an evening boat ride.

"He's not cooperating," I said through gritted teeth as I tried to drag Mauser toward the dock. The more anxious and excited we were, the more Mauser didn't want to go toward the boat.

"I'm not leaving him. Duncan will shoot him out of spite," Dad insisted.

I tossed the leash to Dad, who started pulling while I got behind Mauser and pushed. "No man left behind, dumbass," I said, giving it my all.

We had managed to get to the dock just as we heard the patrol cars screech to a stop in our driveway. As we pushed and shoved our way toward the boat, something next door caught my eye.

On the Leonards' dock I saw a figure running toward their boat, then there was a flash and the sound of a gunshot.

I saw the runner go off the dock and into the water.

The timing was perfect for us. It startled Mauser enough that his muscles relaxed, enabling us to finally shove him off of the dock and into the boat.

"Who's shooting?" Dad asked. He'd been so busy trying to encourage Mauser that he hadn't noticed the murderous tableaux going on next door.

"Someone is shooting at the Leonards," I said, tossing Dad a life vest as I slipped mine on.

"Put one on Mauser, too," Dad said, feeling under the dock for the key to the boat that Dave kept hidden in small key safe. "Got it!"

I had managed to wrestle Mauser into a vest, wondering if it would do any good. Glancing over at the Leonards' dock, I saw Klein in the moonlight holding a large rifle. He saw me too.

Dad turned the key and the engine roared to life. I got the stern line undone and ran for the bow line.

"Klein's over there with a rifle!" I shouted to Dad as I started untying the bow line. Behind us, I could hear shouts and saw deputies streaming around the house. "Go!"

Dad threw the engine in reverse, almost rolling me off the front of the boat. A shot rang out and I heard it whiz close overhead. I ducked down and looked at the other dock. Klein was already jumping down into the Leonards' boat. *Please, God, let the key be well hidden*, I prayed, but the Leonards' boat roared to life just as the deputies came running out onto our dock.

"Get down. Hold on to Mauser!" Dad yelled, pushing the throttle as far forward as it would go.

"Green on the right!" I shouted, pointing to a channel marker.

"I got it, I got it!"

I looked back and could see the white wake and hull of the Leonards' boat. It was bigger than Dave's, but was it faster? After a minute I had my answer as the boat gained a few yards every ten seconds. I didn't bother trying to figure out how long we had before he caught up with us. I just took my Glock from its holster and made sure I had a full magazine and a round in the chamber. I re-holstered and went up to Dad.

"Where's your gun?"

"Hip," he said, keeping both hands on the wheel.

"He's gaining on us pretty fast." I reached around and pulled his Colt Commander out to check it. "I hope you don't regret having only eight rounds," I said, trying to joke, but it came out flat, making my stomach churn. Mauser had wisely spread out in the well of the boat, giving him as much stability as a dog his size could have.

Klein was only a hundred feet behind us now. What would he do? Try and ram us? The boat was planing so much that he would have to slow down to take a shot. I pulled my gun, wondering if it would do any good. Unfortunately, planing the way he was, I couldn't get a shot at him either. I'd just have to wait and see what he did.

I looked toward the front of the boat, trying to see if there was anywhere for Dad to go that would give us an advantage. As I watched, I noticed that Dad was letting the boat ease to the right, getting closer and closer to one of the channel markers. The pole, twice the diameter of a telephone pole, was coming dangerously close. I thought I knew what Dad was planning and I hoped he knew what he was doing.

When we were about twenty yards from the marker, I looked back. Klein's hull was only fifteen yards away.

"Brace yourselves!" Dad yelled.

Just as it seemed we would pass on the inside of the marker, Dad turned the wheel right and then left and we came within a foot of hitting the pole. I looked back and saw Klein swerve at the last second. He wasn't quick enough and I heard a loud smack as the boat clipped the marker. He swerved and lost speed for a moment, but was soon aimed at us again. Dad had bought us a little time, but not much.

In the distance, I saw a light in the sky zig-zagging back and forth. The light was still a long way away, but I was pretty sure what it was. I took out my phone and called 911. Klein was getting close again as I tried to get the dispatcher to understand who I was and what our situation was. I didn't blame her for being slow on the uptake. This was a little out of the ordinary, even for a dispatcher who'd heard everything.

Finally she agreed to connect me with the helicopter that was approaching. Of course, it had been dispatched to find us. Duncan had told them that we were the ones who were armed and dangerous.

The pilot of the helicopter wasn't as sharp as the ones we usually worked with from the Leon County Sheriff's Office. His only advice was to head to the nearest dock and surrender to authorities.

Dad tried the ship-to-shore radio and got the same advice. No one seemed to care that, by the time the authorities showed up, Klein would have killed us. Truth was, they weren't buying our story.

Having exhausted my arguments, I finally hung up. We were in danger of being rammed by Klein again and I doubted Dad's maneuver would work a second time.

"I'm going into the shallows! With luck, we aren't drawing as much water as he is!" Dad shouted.

I tried to picture what would happen if we both ended up stranded on a sandbar. Klein had a rifle while we just had handguns. Not really a fair fight, and fiberglass hulls don't provide hard cover, only concealment. But our options were narrowing fast.

"There's another boat up there. I don't want to take a chance of any bystanders getting hurt," Dad said and started his turn into the shallows.

Behind us, Klein slowed down only a little. Dad kept it at full throttle, risking us bottoming out on something in the shallower water. I looked out and saw that the third boat wasn't sticking to the channel, but seemed to be heading toward us.

"Don't get in too shallow," I told Dad, tapping him on

the shoulder and pointing out the other boat.

"Who do you think that is?"

"Not an innocent bystander. Either a friend or foe!" I shouted back

Klein was ignoring the other boat. He had to have seen it, but he'd apparently decided that taking us out was his number one priority. It was unfolding like a movie where I saw all the action points coming together, but I had no idea how it was going to end.

The other boat wasn't slowing down. Now it was clear that its target was Klein's boat. Seconds from collision, Klein yanked back on the throttle. Apparently, he wasn't a champion chicken player. His move came just a moment too late. The other boat caught the bow of Klein's, whirling it around spectacularly. The other boat had physics on its side and just bounced hard. There was a sickening crunch from its bow, and when it came down from the crest of our wake, a large cracking sound echoed across the water.

I looked back at Klein's boat and couldn't see anyone on it. The boat itself was listing with the motor making an unhealthy grumbling sound as it puttered around in a circle. One of the large outboards had been torn from its mount by the centrifugal force.

Dad pulled the throttle back and was swinging us around at a more leisurely pace. I looked for the other boat and saw it listing heavily in the shallow waters where its trajectory had carried it. I pointed to it and Dad nodded as I got out a light and shined it on the boat. I saw enough of the boat's decal to realize it was Pelican Island's police boat. Someone on board was waving to us.

"Wow, that was exciting!" Sullivan shouted.

His boat was totaled. We helped him over to ours just as the spotlight from the helicopter hit us. We waved, having put away all our guns, while Mauser barked and growled at the loud noise in the sky.

After much negotiation, we came ashore. Turned out that,

during all the fracas, Sheriff Duncan had hit one of his own sergeants with the butt of a rifle. He was arrested and an emergency call to the governor resulted in a temporary suspension for Duncan and the appointment of an acting sheriff.

Major Perkins proved himself a better law enforcement officer in two hours than Duncan had ever been. His men had pulled Bob Leonard from the water and found his wife hiding in a small safe room they had built under a staircase. Bob was unhurt, but badly shaken. With their testimony, Sullivan's and ours, a full manhunt was initiated for Blake Klein. Perkins also agreed to have Jerome released in the morning.

Dad called Mrs. Peters and gave her the good news. She assured him that she'd be there to pick Jerome up and take him home.

"The tide was going out at the time. The current in the channel could take a body ten miles off the coast in an hour," a Coast Guard officer informed us. "We'll continue to look for Klein, but my guess is that he's dead and we'll most likely never recover his body."

Once back on dry land and safely in the house with Dad and Mauser, I texted Cara with some of the evening's more interesting moments. I'd called her right after we'd rescued Sullivan so she wouldn't worry if she heard about it on the news, but I hadn't had time to go into details.

When I opened the text messages I saw the earlier one she'd sent with the addresses. What were they? Then I remembered the camera in my bedroom. Where had Klein stored all that footage? Was finding Klein's archived videos one of the tasks that Pauline had hired Fowler for?

Now I desperately wanted to find it too. I had a restless night thinking about all the blackmail material that might get turned over to someone else if I couldn't find it. Most blackmailers at least threaten that they have a Dead Man's Trigger that will destroy the victim if they kill their tormentor. Some are bluffing, others are not. I didn't see

Klein as a bluffer when it came to ruining other people's lives.

In my tortured thoughts, I imagined a system where all of Klein's material would be instantly posted to some public Internet site. The thought that private images of people I cared about might become part of the great World Wide Web was upsetting. Embarrassing pictures wouldn't help Dad's reelection.

I was up at first light Wednesday morning and called my partner, Darlene Marks.

"I hope you're on your way to work," she said.

"I'm not sure I'll be in this morning."

"I saw all that on the news. Guess they're still debriefing you." Her voice was more sympathetic.

"You know Lionel in IT pretty good, right?"

"Sure, we're friends. I put in a good word when he applied for his job."

"This is important. If you needed someone who could be discreet, would Lionel qualify?"

"I have no idea what you're getting at, but I'd trust him. I've never seen him gossip or stab anyone in the back."

"Is he the kind of guy that could bend a rule?"

"Okay, now. I just told you that we're friends. I'm not going to tell tales on him. Is this some kind of test?" She sounded confused and I couldn't blame her.

"No. I'm sorry, but it wouldn't do either of us any good if I explained the situation. But I need an IT guy who can be discreet."

"Okay, sure. I'd recommend Lionel. Are you in some kind of trouble?"

"Really, Darlene, I can't tell you any more." I thanked her and assured her that I'd be home soon.

I heard Dad moving around downstairs and went to talk to him.

"Come on. We need to pack up and hit the road," he said when he saw me.

"Dad, I need to ask you for a favor. A big one."

"What?" he asked with a puzzled smile.

"I need you to let me stay down here for another day."

"Why?"

"I can't tell you."

"Are you trying to push my buttons?" he said, but when he saw my expression he added, "You aren't, are you? Tell me what it's about. I'm assuming you have a good reason."

"Yes, sir. But I can't tell you." I wasn't about to involve him in what I was planning to do.

"You're being stubborn."

"Just trust me and let me do this," I begged.

"How are you planning to get home?"

"I'll figure that out. Please?"

"You're putting me in an awkward position." One thing he'd told me when I joined the department was that he would never give me any special treatment.

"If anyone else at work asked, would you do it for them?" I reasoned.

He thought about it for a moment. "Anyone but Emerson. That is the laziest, most good-for-nothing… Okay, sure, take the day off. But I can promise you that if you aren't at your desk tomorrow morning by eight o'clock, your two weeks' notice will be back-dated to last Monday."

He wasn't joking.

When Dad left, I called Lionel. I hoped he had some time-off coming and would be willing to expend it for a favor. A favor for someone he'd known only a little over a month.

"Lionel, this is Larry Macklin." I wished I'd taken the time to get to know him a bit better before now. "I've got a big favor to ask of you."

"Sure, what's up? I heard about all the excitement down on the coast. Pete said you all were showing the guys down there how to screw up a murder investigation." He chuckled.

I wasn't surprised that they had already heard details of the night's excitement. The first responder grapevine was pretty efficient.

"Pete's a card," I said dryly. "Look, would you be able to take a personal day and come down here and help me out with a personal matter?" I decided I might as well just blurt it out. The sooner he gave me his answer, the quicker I'd know what I had to do next.

"A personal day? This doesn't have to do with work?"

"No. It's off the books." *Way off the books*, I thought.

"Look, if you just want me to take a look at your computer, I don't mind. It shouldn't take a whole day."

"No. I need you down here. On Pelican Island. This doesn't have anything to do with my computer. I know it's a huge request and that it's coming from someone who's not even a close friend. But I'll find a way to repay you." I was getting dangerously close to begging.

"If you tell me what it is, then I could tell you what you'll need to do. I worked at a call center. I'm pretty good at talking people through stuff," he said reasonably. I didn't want to tell him that I didn't think it would be a good idea to handle this over cell phones.

"I can't go into details. I'm... asking... No, I'm begging for your help."

"No, no. It's not that big of a deal. If you need me, you need me. I'll do it. I never get sick and don't have kids, so the personal days are there."

"Thank you!"

"Hey, don't thank me yet. Who knows if I can even do what you need done."

I gave him directions to Dave's and he said to give him two hours.

CHAPTER TWENTY-FOUR

"So what is this all about?" Lionel asked once we were ensconced at the dining room table. His eyes were narrowed, but there was an impish smile on his dark face as though he expected me to say that we were staging some hilarious prank.

"First, I need your advice. Let's say I was collecting a lot of video and audio recordings that I would need to store in a safe place away from my house. How would I do it? What would it... I don't know, look like?" I asked, feeling very much out of my element.

"What are we talking about here? Is this NSA-level, collecting hundreds of thousands of phone calls, or are we talking one person monitoring his house and wanting to store all the data?" His professional interest was taking over.

"In between. Say if a security company was monitoring thirty houses and wanted to store all the data."

"Is it 24/7? High definition? How many cameras in each house? There are a lot of parameters."

"Think averages, because I don't really know the answers. Or give me high and low. And the cameras might only work when someone is present."

"More surveillance than security. Okay, it would be a

good size, but not ginormous these days. Wherever it is, it would be sucking down some power here in Florida, because you'd want to keep the servers cool. You'd also want it up at least one story in case of a storm surge or any kind of flooding."

"The power," I said thoughtfully. "I've got five addresses."

I pulled the list from Cara's text and we went to Google Earth on my laptop and looked at all of them.

"I'd narrow it down to these two," Lionel said. Both were older buildings. One was two stories and the other three. They'd probably been used for storing tobacco or cotton back in the day. Now their windows were bricked over. "If you can pull up the power records for them, whichever one is sucking down the gigawatts is your target. Actually, let's go from street view to satellite. There, see the shining squares on the roof of this one? Those look like large air conditioning units. And right there. That little white circle could be a satellite dish."

I nodded, then stopped and looked at him. *Can I really trust him?* I asked myself. Normally, trust is based on instinct, but I wanted this to be a very conscious decision on my part.

"From this point on, I need you to agree to several conditions," I finally said.

He shook his head. "I hope you don't think I'm stupid. I heard this guy you all chased down was probably blackmailing people. So what you're looking for is where he stored a bunch of hidden camera footage. Stuff he was using on these people."

"I'm sorry. You're exactly right."

"I'm assuming that since we're here alone, you aren't collecting it for evidence."

"No, I'm not. We don't need it to prosecute the man who did this. The State has more than enough evidence. All it would do if it got out would be to injure people. I don't know if they are innocent people or not. I suspect a lot of them are."

Right then, I realized something. Klein didn't want to target real criminals. He wanted people who had old secrets. If he'd targeted someone who was currently committing crimes, then there would be the chance that the bad guy would get caught. If he did, he'd rat out Klein. Klein wanted to get secrets on basically good people. *What a rat!* I thought.

I considered my next words, but Lionel deserved to know all of my motivations. "The sheriff and I, along with our girlfriends, stayed in this house this weekend. It's one of the ones that this guy monitored."

"Ouch. That's not good. I had a girlfriend whose ex posted some of her private pictures. She was really damaged by that."

"Exactly."

"You want it all destroyed?"

"Yep. What I'm doing is illegal as hell, but I think it's the right thing to do. If anything goes wrong, and we get caught now or later, I'll do what I can to protect you. But I'll be so deep in the hole I doubt I'll be able to help you."

"My dad was in the Army. He always said that when he was on a battlefield, the rules simply didn't exist. Every decision you made had to be weighed by whether it was a decision you thought was right and if you'd feel justified in your actions. I asked him how he knew the answer. Dad said it usually came down to whether you were helping more or less people by your actions. I think I'd be helping more people by helping you."

"What are we going to need?"

"I guess we want to do it as fast as possible."

"Without burning the building down."

"That wouldn't guarantee anything. You can recover a lot of data from a server that's been in a fire. No, I just need a crowbar and a couple of good drills."

Klein had literally built a building within a building. The original building was comprised of two stories with open floorplans. On the second floor, Klein had built a concrete block room that was thirty feet by twenty feet. After we pried our way through the interior door, we found a gleaming white room cooled down to sixty-eight degrees with several dozen servers purring inside. They didn't take up as much of the room as I thought they would. There was a good half of the room still available. Klein had a couch, an HD TV and a couple of computer consoles and monitors set up in the open area.

"He took care of himself," Lionel said, looking at a refrigerator stocked with beer and snacks that sat in the corner by the couch.

"Let's get to work."

Lionel showed me how to pry open the backs of the servers and rip out the hard drives. We piled them up and then drilled holes in all of them.

"What a shame. There's about sixty thousand dollars' worth of equipment here."

"We need to hurry. I don't know how hard the sheriff's office is looking for this place. Luckily, without Klein they might not even think of it."

"What'd he do, exactly?"

"From the people we talked to last night and what we'd already figured out, I think he found out that one of his marks had hired a private eye to to find this place so that they could get out from under his thumb."

"Ballsy."

"She seemed like a pretty straight-shooting old woman. I wouldn't doubt she knew that there were other people he was victimizing. I could see her wanting to help all of them. Anyway, Klein found out, snuck up behind the private eye she'd hired and clobbered him in the back of the head with a pipe or something. The private eye fell into the bottom of a boat and drowned in the bilge water."

"Did Klein mean to kill him?"

"I'm sure he planned on killing him. He might not have expected him to drown while he was lying in the bottom of the boat, but either way, Klein took the body and dumped it at the house of one of his blackmail victims as a warning to them all."

"Did he kill the couple too? And what about the old lady?" Lionel asked, raising his voice to be heard over the drills.

"Mrs. Schultz killed herself. Fernandez heard about the private eye and decided to issue his own warning to Klein. He went to his house and tried to ambush him in the garage. I don't know if he intended to kill him or if he was just hoping to scare Klein off."

"So Klein killed them?"

"From the crime scene, I'd say Klein set up a meeting with them. The house looked like they were just pacing around, waiting for him to show up. They'd even told the neighbors that they were going to be out of town so that no one else would bother them. Klein must have offered them something. Maybe he pretended that the shooting had really frightened him, and he was promising to give them the blackmail material back. Why did they trust him? Who knows? Maybe they were going to try and get the drop on Klein when he came over and kill him themselves. Whatever they'd planned failed. Klein got the upper hand and killed both of them and then tried to make it look like a robbery and rape."

"Wow."

We finished destroying all of the hard drives and anything else in the room that looked like it could store information. After that, we cut the cable running to the satellite dish on the roof.

"I hate to say it, but if this guy was as rich, evil and determined as you make him sound, he probably stored the information somewhere else as a backup."

"We'll have to take that chance. With him dead, if it exists, hopefully no one else will know how to access it."

I bought him a late lunch before we headed back to Adams County.

That night, back in my own living room with Ivy on my lap,

Cara cuddled up next to me and Alvin curled up at her feet, I knew that I'd done the right thing destroying those servers.

"Did you have a good vacation?" Cara asked snarkily, which led to a vicious tickle battle that disturbed both Ivy and Alvin.

"I don't think I could handle another vacation like that. Like Dorothy said, there's no place like home."

"I just have one question," Cara said when we'd settled down again. "I know what everyone's secret was except for the Holdens and Judith Murray."

"I don't know what Judith's was. I suspect it was her husband's anyway. Probably had to do with a crooked deal." I was willing to leave things there, but Cara's curiosity was sparked.

"So you know what the Holdens' is?"

"You should probably just drop it."

"Come on, what is it? I won't tell," she prodded me.

I gave in. "Okay, turns out that Mrs. Holden was married to another man before she married Ed."

"That's not a big deal."

"Actually she's still technically married to this other man. She was in a cult and Ed helped her escape. Plus the cult is still active and the members are reportedly vengeful and mean as snakes. They have a tendency to hunt down people who try to escape, so the Holdens had to hide. This also meant that Jessica never got an official divorce."

Cara's phone rang. "It's Genie," Cara said and answered it. "Hey! Yes, he's recovering. How's Ted? What? No, we haven't. Okay, we will. Thanks." Cara put down her phone. "Where's your laptop?"

In a few minutes we had my laptop up and running. Cara told me what to search for and soon the web gurus had delivered up a YouTube video that had been shared to the Adams County Sheriff's Office's Facebook page among other places. Clicking on it revealed Jerome sitting on a couch in Mrs. Peters's house. I hit the play button.

"Hi, I'm Jerome Martel. I want to tell everyone about a

good friend of mine. Sheriff Ted Macklin of Adams County. What?" he said to someone off camera.

Mrs. Peters's voice said, *"Don't forget his son."*

"I wouldn't. Larry. My good friend Sheriff Ted Macklin and his son Mr. Larry. If it wasn't for them, I wouldn't be here. I was in jail. Another sheriff made me say things that weren't true and wouldn't let me go and lied to me. He lied to me a lot. Jail was really, really bad. Most of the people were mean and only a couple didn't yell at me or hit me. See." He turned his head back and forth to show a couple of purple and yellow bruises that were severe enough to show through his dark complexion.

"The bad sheriff told me I'd killed the best friend I ever had, Mr. Fowler. Mr. Fowler had given me a computer and some tools and stuff but the bad sheriff, his name is Sheriff Duncan, lied and lied, saying I killed him and that I'd hit him with a pipe and he drowned in an old boat on Mr. Fowler's place. I wouldn't ever hurt Mr. Fowler. But Sheriff Duncan said that I did and that if I didn't say I did it, then I'd go to jail until they hooked me up to Ol' Sparky and electrocuted me. I was super scared. But I had a good guy on my side.

"Mrs. Peters, she's my other best friend, says that God sent Sheriff Macklin to help us. I think that's about right. He's like some hero on the television. Better 'cause he's real. I wish he could be *our* sheriff. Anyway, Mrs. Peters says that Sheriff Macklin has to be elected again or something. I told her that I wanted to help him win and be sheriff again, so she got her nephew to come over and help me do this. I think you'd be crazy not to vote for him. That's what I wanted to say. He found the bad guy and got me out of jail, even though it wasn't his job. Mrs. Peters says that some people just do good things and that's how Sheriff Macklin is. If you want a real good sheriff, then keep Sheriff Macklin. Thank you, Sheriff Macklin, you're my hero." The video ended with Jerome giving a thumbs up.

"Wow! That's great." I chuckled, not at Jerome's performance, which had come off as warm and genuine, but at the idea of Dad as a superhero. "Dad's a bit of a hero, I guess. But he's also a bit of a horse's ass sometimes," I joked.

"Look at the views," Cara said, pointing to a number solidly in the five digits. "And he just posted that this afternoon."

We clicked over to a local news website to see if there was any update on the search for Klein's body. The search was still ongoing, but I could tell by the clips that the Coast Guard and sheriff's office didn't expect to find anything and were working hard to lower expectations.

"I'd feel better if they found his body," Cara said.

"I'm sure he's dead and washed out to sea. Anyway, I'm tired, and if I'm even two minutes late in the morning, Dad said I'm fired."

Cara raised her eyebrows at me, her expression making it clear that she'd decided Dad was all bark and no bite. I grinned and pulled her close to me, kissing her cheek.

"Maybe you're right," I said. "But I think I'll play it safe, just in case."

Larry Macklin returns in:

July's Trials
A Larry Macklin Mystery–Book 9

ACKNOWLEDGMENTS

The usual thanks go out to my wife, Melanie, for her editing skills and support; and to H. Y. Hanna for her inspiration, assistance and encouragement.

And I'm especially grateful for all the fans of the series—thank you for reading. I hope you continue to enjoy Larry's adventures!

Original Cover Concept by H. Y. Hanna
Cover Design by Florida Girl Design, Inc.
www.gobookcoverdesign.com

ABOUT THE AUTHOR

A. E. Howe lives and writes on a farm in the wilds of North Florida with his wife, horses and more cats than he can count. He received a degree in English Education from the University of Georgia and is a produced screenwriter and playwright. His first published book was *Broken State*. The Larry Macklin Mysteries is his first series and he released a new series, the Baron Blasko Mysteries, in summer 2018. The first book in the Macklin series, *November's Past*, was awarded two silver medals in the 2017 President's Book Awards, presented by the Florida Authors & Publishers Association; the ninth book, *July's Trials*, was awarded two silver medals in 2018. Howe is a member of the Mystery Writers of America, and was co-host of the "Guns of Hollywood" podcast for four years on the Firearms Radio Network. When not writing, Howe enjoys riding, competitive shooting and working on the farm.

Made in the USA
Columbia, SC
22 April 2025

56999985R00136